A ROSE
ON THE
CONCRETE COURT

ROYCE DIXON SR.

S.H.E. PUBLISHING, LLC

A Rose on the Concrete Court

ISBN: 978-1-964061-30-6
Library of Congress Control Number: 2025938515

This is a work of fiction. Names, characters, businesses, places, events, and incidents are either the products of the author's imagination or used in a fictitious manner. Any resemblance to actual persons, living or dead, or actual events is purely coincidental.

Cover design by: Nabin Karna
Interior design and layout by: Nabin Karna

Published by SHE Publishing LLC
Indianapolis, Indiana
www.shepublishingllc.com
info@shepublishingllc.com

Printed in the United States of America
First Edition: April 2025

TABLE OF CONTENTS

This page is intentionally left blank

A ROSE ON THE CONCRETE COURT

Growing up in the hood, all the guys on our block dreamt of making it big in either football, baseball or basketball. That was our American dream; to do that, you had to play in the parks. That is where your name was made, and pretty much where you could find our pops, AJ Rose! He was six-foot-three, one-hundred eighty-five lbs. of lean muscle. He could shoot from wherever he set his feet and all you would hear was the chains singing. They say he had one of the sweetest jumpers you could ever see. His handles were ridiculous. He would have the ball on a string and could do anything with it. Fans would come from all over town to watch him play and 'Pop' would put on a show- dribbling, shooting and of course, he had the hops to go with all his other abilities; you better not put the ball in front of him or have a weak hand. Before you knew it, he would be on the other end of the court with a spectacular dunk and a wink. For some unknown reason, that was his thing. He would steal the ball, get the dunk and then wink at you as if to say *yea I got you, now what?* When he would give that wink, all the ladies would go crazy. I think that's why he did it more than anything. He loved to get the ladies excited. That's how he met my mom. Whenever and wherever he played, my mom would sometimes be there watching in amazement. She was fifteen at the time when she first saw my dad playing ball. She and her girlfriends would walk up to the park and just hang out, watching all the guys play ball. At first, she says she didn't notice my dad, that he was just another baller, but she quickly learned who AJ Rose was after he hit a three from just passed the half-court line. She says it was one of those moments when you lock eyes with someone from across the room and you give them that certain look that only that one special person can give you and then he winked at her. After that, it was over with; she knew then that there was something special about him, or so she thought. Every day after that, she would follow Pops around town to watch him play ball, and in every game, he would hit a three and then point to her like *yea, that one was for you.* Her heart would melt. Then after the game, he would kiss her before they got into his car and drive off to the next pickup game.

Over the summer, the nights grew longer, and Mom was staying out later and later, until my grandmother found out that she was dating an older guy with a car. Grandpa wasn't having it. He told her that she had to leave Pops alone, immediately. He didn't want his daughter dating some grown man and staying out all night riding around in his car. "You ain't got no business being with a grown man in his car after dark. He's too old for you and too mature for you. What does some nineteen-year-old man want with a fifteen-year-old girl?" As the old folks say, I guess Mom had 'started smelling herself and was too big for her britches', because the more they told her not to hang with Pops, the more she did. She started hanging out even more and then skipping school to be with him. Her grades started slipping and she started drinking and smoking weed. There was no turning back for Mom at this point. She was head over heels in love, and no one could tell her anything; and then it happened…PREGNANT at 16. She was terrified to tell my grandparents. She tried to hide it for a while, but that didn't last long. Even the oversized clothes couldn't hide the fact that she was pregnant. When she first told Pops about it, he denied it. He was a sophomore in college with aspirations of playing in the league. The thought of having a baby was the last thing he wanted to hear. Eventually, he came around, but their relationship would never be the same. He started cheating with other women and lying about anything and everything. Although he never said that Mom trapped him per se. He would crack little jokes like "he fell for the old banana in the tail pipe." Mom was in a no-win situation. She had been lying to Grandma and Grandpa, skipping school and now pregnant with TWINS! Grandpa snapped and kicked her out of the house. He couldn't stand the lying and how disrespectful she had gotten. She moved from place to place for a while before Pops eventually let her stay in his apartment. It was a small one-bedroom studio apartment with a small kitchen and a makeshift living room with folded walls to separate the kitchen from the living room. He didn't have much, but that's what he liked about it. Everything was cost-effective. A card table for a dining room table, and some lawn chairs for a sofa. Since he was hardly ever there. It was low maintenance, to say the least.

Shortly after Mom moved in, Pops hurt his knee in a pickup game that he shouldn't have been playing in and tore his knee up. Total reconstruction. In his mind, he was finished, the scholarship-gone, extra cash from the boosters- gone, everything that was going right for him was now GONE! This sent Pops clean off. He was on the downward slope to nowhere. He did not care about anything and no one, not even my mother! All he wanted to do was drink, smoke and gamble. He was always trying to catch that quick buck, but when that did not work, he would use different women to get what he wanted. Pops could talk the panties off any woman; he was smooth! Mom tried to work, but she would often quit or get fired because she would either oversleep or be late getting to work because she did not have a car. Times got hard for them at this point. To make things worse, Mom was in the advanced stages of her pregnancy and started having contractions. Pops was not anywhere to be found. Luckily, Sissy, who lived next door, was home and heard Mom screaming in pain. She got to the hospital just in time, and soon after, we were born. Twin boys, Aaron & Jamal Rose, two 'six pounds, seven ounces' identical twins. Aaron came out first. We were born 10 minutes apart. I guess I wanted to spend a little more time with Mom; at least that is what she says to me all the time.

Now, Aaron has always been the twin that does things first and I'd just tag along with him. If he messed up, I was the one who tried to clean up after him. He has never really followed rules, and he always seemed to get by on his charm. He was much like Pops in that regard, a straight charmer. When he would get in trouble at school, he would turn on the charm to show his dimples and the teachers always gave him another chance. I, on the other hand, was quieter and more reserved. I sat back and observed people; l would listen to what they had to say, but then I would watch their actions to see how they moved. That often told me what I needed to know about that person. This was a skill that I worked on daily with Aaron. He would often try to BS me, but I could always tell when he was lying to me. He did not realize it, but his lips would twitch when he lied. That was always more telling when he was not talking, which wasn't that often.

These last 16 years have been up and down for the most part. When things were good, they were good and when things got bad, they were so bad. It all depended on how good Pops was hustling. He was hardly ever home with us; he would be out getting money and then come back and shower us with gifts like shoes, jewelry, clothes and things like that. However, when things got tight and he was not making any money, he would come home and get drunk and high for days on end, and when he was under the influence, he would get so angry and mean. He would punch us and tell us how we needed to man up. Then he would take it out on Mom. They never fought in front of us, but we could hear them behind the doors and then later we would see the bruises on Mom's face and her body. We did not understand at first, but as we grew older, we began to know what was going on. I always wanted to help, but Aaron would tell me to stay out of it and if we got in the way, Pops would not buy us anything anymore or he would take it out on us. So, to escape the drama, we would go up to the park and play ball. This was our safe place, our sanctuary. We could go there and stay for hours, even if it was just the two of us. Some say we were just naturally gifted at it and that basketball was in our blood. We would always hear the stories of how good Pops was back in the day. We took pride in that. We worked hard at being just like him in that regard. Day and night, we would be there putting in work so our name would be known throughout the city just like Pop was. We were getting there too. From the time we were about 12 years old, we would dominate the courts. No one in the city could touch us when it came to hooping.

It got to the point where we had to play with the adult men to get a good game in or we would just play each other. Out of the two of us, Aaron would always get the best of me, but he would also say that I was fouling him or traveling, anything that would give him an edge or the ball back. I would let him get away with it just because I did not want to have a confrontation with him. It was bad enough at the house, so I did not want to take that to the basketball court. He thrived on the bickering. Even when we played against the men at the park, he would talk trash or try to embarrass whoever was guarding him.

The same way we acted on the court, was the same way we acted when we were at school. We got a lot of respect from people because of what we did on the court. The teachers and the girls loved us and the guys either feared us or hated us; Aaron more so than me, since I was the quiet twin. Schoolwork was easy for Aaron as well, but me, not so much. I struggled in class and would often have to either stay late to get extra help or have Aaron go to my class for me to pass a test or help get my work done. We pulled the old twin switch thing a couple of times on our teachers. Sometimes I think they knew, but didn't say anything because they wanted to make sure we stayed eligible to play for the school.

Up to this point, we had won three State titles back-to-back-to-back. This twenty-twenty-five season we were up for our forth State Championship. We have been playing all over the country and now we were getting national attention. Everywhere we played, we sold out of the gyms. This bothered me because I did not want anyone to see what was going on behind the scenes and how we were living.

Aaron thrived in it! The more attention, the better. As much as I could, I stayed in the shadows and truly had little to say on camera. If I had to pinpoint a time in our lives when things began to turn for us, I would have to say that this was it.

As the fame grew, we started receiving money from guys in the neighborhood; everywhere we went, we would get free food and then we started playing against guys for money. Something we should have never started doing. Guys would bet hundreds of dollars on us and against us.

One day, we were at the park just messing around and this black van pulled up on us. It was Big Nick. He was one of the local gang leaders who lived in the neighborhood that we lived in. He would look out for us from time to time to make sure we were eating and being taken care of. He and Pops were bout the same age and they used to ball together and hustle together back in the day until Pops tore up his knee. He gets out of the van and calls us over to talk. When we got to the van, one of his guys opened the side door and inside, we could see boxes on top of boxes of Jordans and two duffle bags filled with money. "What you think about this fellas? It's all for you. You can have all of this IF you make sure that in your next game, we don't cover the spread of ten points. I got a lot of money riding on y'all to win, but not to cover the spread. All you have to do is miss a shot or two here and there, make a bad pass or whatever you need to do, just don't cover the spread. That's it, simple," Big Nick says. "Man, I'm with it Aaron quickly jumps in. We get all of this, and we can still win. That's a no-brainer to me. We got you!" Aaron yelps. "Jamal, come here Bro. We need to talk!" I say to him. "Talk about what Bro? This is easy money. Did you see all that cash and those shoes? Bro…we can get out of that nasty apartment and eat good; not to mention we will be looking good in the new J's, we are getting this money," Aaron defends. "Bro, you are not thinking. This could ruin our college careers before we even get started," I insisted, "Not to mention this is illegal. Aaron, if we get caught, we could go to prison. We were not built for that. Bro come on you tripping." Aaron holds a steady gaze and says, "Look Jamal, we beat the brakes off this team the last time. All we have to do is keep it close. Nobody will know unless you or I talk. We know Big Nick won't say anything. This is easy money bro. We are doing this. Now stop tripping. I'll talk, you just chill." Without hesitation, I say, "Bro I'm not with this, I'm out." "Jamal, you just gone leave all this money and leave me hanging?" Aaron begs. "Bro, we don't have to do this. We can just walk away," I say to him. "Jamal, that's too much money to walk away from," Aaron replies. "Well, you do what you need to do; as for me? I'm gone." Aaron is flabbergasted. "Bro we ain't never ditched one another, I can't believe you doing this to me. We can help Mom and Pops by doing this," he argued. "Bro I'm gone, I'm out!" Big Nick started to scream at us, "Aaaayyy, what y'all gone do?" "Here we come," Aaron replies. Big Nick was getting impatient, "Man, what's up? We going to do this or what? "Yea, big fella, we got you," Aaron tries convincing him. "What do you mean we? I only see you!" "I mean Jamal is just a little nervous, but I will talk to him. He will be straight. Don't even trip!" Aaron says. "Ok, but I'm telling you now. DON'T MESS WITH MY MONEY!!! If you do, I'm going to do something to you, him, your momma and daddy! AM I CLEAR!?" Big Nick fumes. "Bro don't trip, I got you. You can drive the van back to your spot and just leave it out front, somebody will pick it up later," Aaron says. "Remember what I said, we can't win by more than ten points," Big Nick reminds him. "Bro, I got you. Don't trip!!!"

"Aaron, where have you been? Big Nick's goons have been circling the block for hours now. I thought something had happened to you," I press when Aaron finally arrives home. "I went shopping bro, and I was waiting for Mom to go to work so I could bring in the cash and the shoes. While I was waiting, I went on a little shopping spree. Check this out." "DANG Bro, where did you get that ice from?" That go hard!" Aaron replies, "I went to the Jewelers, flashed a little cash and this is what they produced. I had them make you one too. This one is for you. Open it up! This is a one-carrot red and white diamond pendant wrapped in platinum gold." "Bro this is dope! I love how they put the rose on the basketball," I reply. Aaron pauses, "Wait, I thought you didn't want to have anything to do with this. You walked away remember, leaving me hanging." "Bro, I'm sorry, but it just didn't feel right to me," Jamal explains. "Hustling on the court is one thing, but this is something different. Not to mention you know Big Nick and his crew are crazy. You know what they did to T-bone and old crackhead Willie. These dudes don't play bro, you know this," Jamal defends. "Yea, I know Bro, but that won't be us. This is easy money. Now chill and enjoy this money and these gifts that I just bought us. We are going out for steaks tonight. No more Noodles for us! From now on we are living large and doing it big," Aaron says. "I hear you Bro but how are we going to tell Mom and Pop how we got this money? Pops might be cool with it, but Mom is not," Jamal presses. "Look, all we have to do is tell pops that we won it in a game. He is a hustler, and he knows the game. He can smooth it over with Mom. At the end of the day, we need this money. Now let's get dressed and go eat," Aaron says.

Just as they were getting ready to leave, AJ walks through the door. "Jamal, Aaron get out here now!!" "What up Pops?" "What the hell is this I'm hearing that you guys are working with Big Nick?"AJ screams at the two of them. "What are you talking about Pops?"Aaron replies with a shakey voice. "You know what the fuck

I'm talking about! I was just at the spot, and I overheard them talking about how they had this game in the bag, and then I heard something about some bags of money. Aaron come here… What is this? How did you get this chain and them new J's? Somebody better tell me something quick," AJ demands. "It's like this Pops, I saw an opportunity to make this family some real money, so I took it. It's no different than what you do. You hustle for money, so we did too. We can get out of this apartment, move to somewhere nice and have food in the fridge," Aaron explains. "OH, SO NOW YOU'RE THE MAN OF THE HOUSE! YOU MAKE DECISIONS FOR THE FAMILY HUH!? BOY have you lost your damn mind! I do what I do because for one, I'm grown and two whatever I do… it doesn't put this family in danger. What you did was stupid, and reckless, and now you just put a mark on all of us. What happens if you can't make good on your promise? What happens, Huh?" AJ asks. "Pops that is not going to happen!" Aaron defends. "How do you know? Can you say with one hundred percent certainty that you are going to win that game and keep it under ten points? No, you cannot! No one can do that. Even as good as I was, there was no guarantee. Anything can happen during a game and you and your brother don't control it all. There is only so much you can do!" "Pops, we got this. Look at all this money we got," Aaron says, as he pulls out a wad of bills all rolled up and hands it to his dad. "There are two bags full of money in there and it's ours POPs." Aaron heads over to the refrigerator and opens the door. "Look in there Pops, what do you see? Nothing… you see nothing at all. Some spoiled milk and a half drank bottle of water. What is that going to do for the four of us? Jamal and I have been hustling since middle school, just to eat every day. You're hardly ever here and Mom is out working making pennies. Now we have some real money, and we can eat and get out of here. I get what you're saying Pops and I'm not trying to be disrespectful, but we need this opportunity. I am tired of living like this and so is Jamal, he is just too scared to say anything," Aaron says, pleading his case. "Oh, and you are not scared Huh? You got it all figured out now Huh! You are the man now right? Boy, I ought to…" AJ grabs Aaron by his collar and draws his fist back as if he is going to punch him. Aaron is so scared, his eyes begin to water and his body is paralyzed; he can't move a muscle, and tears begin to roll down his face. Jamal yells, "POPS, Please don't!" AJ drops his fist, lets Aaron go and storms out of the house. Jamal moves closer to check on Aaron, "Bro, are you ok?" "Man, get the hell back. Now, you want to say something? You just stood there and didn't say shit bro! I have never done you like that. Remember when we were in the fourth grade and that bully was picking on you? Who stepped in and had your back? When we were on the court in the sixth grade and that kid kept elbowing you in the post, who stepped in? Me!! I have always had your back, and tonight you leave me hanging not once, but twice." Tears were still rolling down Aaron's face. "Never in a million years would I have ever thought that you would just leave me high and dry. Now I know I can't count on nobody but me." Aaron heads back into the bedroom and begins to pack up his things. "Bro, what are you doing? Where are you going?" Jamal asks. "I'm out of here! I don't need you, or Pops! I'm leaving and I'll make it on my own. I'll be back for my money later, I'm out!" Aaron says as he storms off. "Bro, where are you going?" Jamal presses. "Oh, now you are worried? You should have thought about that earlier today or when Pops was about to smash me. I'm out. You live your life and I'm going to live my best life!" Aaron storms out of the apartment slamming the door. Jamal is at a loss for words, standing in the middle of the bedroom as if he were frozen in time, speechless.

Later that night, Monica finally makes it home from working a double shift. "Aaron, Jamal, I'm home, I brought home some food from work if you guys are hungry. Hey baby, where is your brother?" "Ma, I have some bad news to tell you. Aaron and Pop got into it and he left, he said he was tired of living here, packed a few things and walked out." "What, are you serious? What did they get into it about?" she asks. "Well, Aaron and I were at the park earlier today playing ball and Big Nick rolled up on us with these two huge duffle bags full of cash and a van full of Jordans. I didn't want to take it, but Aaron decided that we should take it." His mom interrupts… "Why would Nick give you all that money? What does he want from the two of you to give you that amount of cash?" "He wants us to point shave the sectional game. He wants us to win it but not by more than ten points so that we don't cover the spread." "Jamal, isn't that illegal? I'm not sure, but I know it's not right." Jamal adds, "The worst part of it is that he said if we didn't do it, he was going to hurt all of us." His mom sizes him up with her eyes, "Are you kidding me? What was your brother thinking?" "I don't know Ma, all he could see was all the cash. He said that we could use the money to move out of this apartment and have some real money until we made it to the league. Then Pops came home, saw all the cash and next thing you know, he was getting loud with Pops and Pops was yelling back at him. The next thing I know- Pop had him by his collar getting ready to punch him. He didn't though, he just let him go and stormed off. Aaron stayed there against the wall for a minute, then we got into an argument because he said I didn't have his back with Big Nick and Pops. He said he was leaving and not coming back. He took some cash and said he would be back to get the rest later," Jamal ended. "So where is the cash now? It's in there, in the room." "Where is it? Show me… Nick gave you all this and these shoes?" "Yeah, and Aaron went out and spent some of the money already and bought us these necklaces," Jamal adds. "OH, my GOD, we can't keep this here. We have to give this money back. We can take the jewelry back in the morning and get the money back and hopefully, your brother hasn't spent too much of the money he took, and I pray your father can pay the rest back. Lord knows I ain't got it." "Mom, I don't think you understand… guys like Big Nick don't take their money back. If we don't do what he wants, he is going to kill us all," Jamal says. "Don't say that, maybe your father can talk to him. They grew up together and he knows how this stuff works. Now go ahead and go to bed. Your father and I will figure this out. Come here and give Momma a hug. You know I love you right?" "Yes, ma'am I know. I love you too Momma!" "Then trust me when I tell you, everything will be OK." "OK Momma," Jamal says.

Monica picks up her cell phone to call AJ. "Hey Baby, it's me. I need you to give me a call. I just talked to Jamal, and he told me that you and Aaron got into it and now he is gone. He said he was tired of being here and that he was going to make it on his own. He also told me that Big Nick gave them some money to throw a game and if they don't, he is going to kill us all. Baby, what are we going to do? I'm scared, call me back as soon as you get this message."

AJ is furious and now scouring the city looking for Big Nick. Going through all the local hang-outs and dope spots, Nick is nowhere to be found. Just as he is about to give up, he picks up his phone and sees that he has a voicemail from Monica. As he is listening to the voicemail, Nick's black van pulls up on him with guns drawn. Nick taps on AJ's window. "I hear you have been looking for me and you are out here being aggressive. What's up?" AJ sees that Nick's guys have him surrounded. "Nick, you already know what it is bro! How are you going to give my kids all that money and shoes to throw a game for you? Bro, you know that can cost them their future." "Man shut up, ain't nobody going to find out unless you tell them, or you do something stupid. Do you know how much money I'm going to make with this? Not to mention I have been taking care of your boys since they have been playing ball. When your crackhead ass was out here bad and your girl was at work, how do you think they were eating? You did not have food at the crib, so I made sure they ate. When they had holes in their shoes, who do you think got them new shoes? You know damn well the school is not giving them that. Hell, I have been more of a father to them than you have and now it's time to collect on my investment. So, I would advise you to take the money, talk to your other son and make sure his bitch ass doesn't do anything stupid and let this thing play out. Otherwise, Mr. AJ Rose, we will be lying roses on four graves! Your boys, your girl and yours! You understand what I'm telling you?" "Yea, I hear you." "AJ, you know me and what I'm capable of, so please don't try me or think you are slick… I got people all over watching you and if you think you are going to try to run to the police, think again, because I got people there too! You were a pretty good point guard back in the day when we played, so you understand the importance of everybody playing their role and running the play. Let this play run out and everybody wins. Otherwise, the only ones that will be losing is your family and I promise you, I will make them suffer while you watch before I kill them and you. One last thing, if you ever come to my spots again looking for me like you did, I will have you killed on the spot! Am I clear?" "Yeah, I got it!"

Nick and his boys get back in the van and peel off. AJ sits in his car furious and begins to reminisce on his past as tears begin to fall. He realizes that all his past indiscretions are coming back to haunt him. Now because of him, his family is in danger and there is nothing he can do to save them. As his anxiety gets worse, his craving to get high increases tremendously. He reaches into the glove compartment to find his stash, but he's out. He begins to search the car frantically and to no avail; it's bone dry, not even an empty baggie with just a trace of cocaine. His hands begin to shake, and his mouth is dry. He reaches into his pockets to see if he has enough money to get him through and his pockets are as empty as the car. He is in full withdrawal mode; the craving is getting so intense that nothing matters at this point. He needs to get a fix, and he needs it now! AJ picks up the phone to call Monica back to see if he can get some money from her. She usually has some cash she gets from tips.

"Hey Baby it's me, I just got your message and I'm out here trying to fix things. I haven't found Aaron yet, but I think I know where Big Nick is. I think he might be at the gambling spot, but to get in, I have to play a few dollars. I got like sixty dollars on me, so if you have about forty, that would be enough to get me in. I think I can talk to Nick and fix all of this, but I need to talk to him tonight," he says to her. "AJ all I have is about fifty dollars and I was going to use that for groceries in the morning," Monica says. "Oh, don't worry Baby, I will be able to double that, I'm sure. The guys that will be there tonight play poker and they are terrible poker players. I'm going to get all of them tonight just like I always do," AJ reassures. "I don't know AJ, this is all we have got and there is nothing in the fridge, the boys will be hungry in the morning, and I want to make sure they have something," Monica rebuts. "Baby don't worry, I got you! Don't I always come through? Am I not a clutch player?" AJ asks. "Yea, but Baby this is all we have!" AJ continues to press, "I know Baby, trust me. I got this." "Well, come back home and get it. I'll leave it on the table, and I'll be in the shower or the bed when you get here. It's been a long day and I'm exhausted," Monica submits. "I'm on my way then. See you in a few minutes," AJ replies.

AJ walks through the door and doesn't see Monica, so he tip-toes through to the kitchen like a thief in the night, grabs the money off the table and sneaks back out without anyone knowing that he had been there. The mission is complete, now he's on his way to go cop a bag to get high. He calls his dealer and tells him he needs two twenty-dollar bags of powder. "AJ, you know you my guy, but you still owe me from the last time, so you better have all my money," the dealer says. "Come on bro, you tripping did you forget who you talking to? Haven't I always paid you? Haven't I always come through for you? Then why are we having this conversation? I said I got you," AJ says. "Well, you know where to meet me," the dealer says. "Bet, I'll be there in ten minutes," AJ responds.

AJ pulls up and gets out to meet his dealer. "First things first, you got my five-hundred you owe me?" the dealer initiates. "Yea, I do but it's not on me per say. I have it but it's at the house, I promise. I do have forty for the two bags though right here in my pocket, see. If you just let me get these two, I can go back and get it and bring it back to you," AJ says. "Have you lost your damn mind AJ!? I told you to have my money, did I not?" the dealer says as he strikes AJ with the butt of his gun, knocking him to the ground. The dealer then begins to beat AJ, punching and kicking him as he lay helplessly on the ground. All he can do is curl up in a ball. He reaches down and takes the forty dollars from AJ and leaves him bleeding on the concrete court at the park.

The next morning AJ finds himself lying in a hospital bed with nurses standing over him. "Where am I?" AJ asks "Sir, you're in the hospital. You were found unconscious and bleeding pretty badly. You have some broken ribs and a mild concussion," the doctor says. "I don't remember any of that. Wait, where is my phone? I need to make a call," AJ says. "Sir, there was no phone on you when they brought you in. You didn't have anything other than your wallet," the doctor replies. "What about my keys?" "No sir, all you had was your wallet!" the doctor says. "FUCK!!! HOW LONG AM I GOING TO BE HERE? I NEED TO GO!" AJ exclaims. "You can leave whenever you feel up to it. All your vitals came back normal," the doctor says. "Ok well, can you get my discharge papers? I have some things I need to take care of," AJ says before leaving.

A little while later, AJ knocks on the door to his apartment. "Who is it?" Monica asks. "It's me." The door slowly opens. Monica gasps when she sees AJ. "What happened to you?" She asks. "I was jumped by a couple of guys at the gambling spot, and they took my car and the money I had won," AJ lied. "AJ that was our grocery shopping money! I needed that for the kids. What are we going to do now?" Monica says. AJ responds, "I don't know Baby… Well Aaron is still gone, and Jamal is still in bed. Look, take a few dollars out of that bag Nick gave the boys and use that to get us by for today and I'll think of something to get it back so we can give it all back to Nick." Monica looks at him surprised, "I don't think that's a good idea, Baby. If we come up one dollar short, Nick will kill us. You know that," she says. "Baby don't worry about that. I'll handle Nick; you just go to the store and handle what you need to," AJ reassures her. "AJ are you sure?" "Yes, do what you have to do, and I'll do what I have to do, and Baby, I'm sorry," AJ says. "Sorry for what? I'm sorry for everything, how I have treated you over the years, for how I have been acting; for this situation I have put us in. I'm so sorry!" AJ breaks down and begins sobbing uncontrollably. "It's OK Baby," Monica tries to reassure him. "No, it's not. I have not been a good man to you or father to our boys. Now, because of me, all of our lives are in danger. One of my sons has picked up my bad habits and the other one is scared of me. Both of them hate me and if I'm honest with myself, I hate me too. I hate the man I've become. I never thought my life would be like this. I was supposed to be playing in the league making millions of dollars and instead, we are in this small two-bedroom apartment with everything scheduled to be cut off. I don't have any money in the bank or in my pockets. What kind of man have I become?" AJ says as he weeps. "AJ, with all your faults, you're still the father of my children and the love of my life. No, we don't have this or that, and life may have dealt you a cruel blow, but as long as we are here together, we still have a chance… AJ, do you mind if I pray for you and over you?" Monica says. He replies, "No, at this point we have nothing left, but prayer." Monica begins to pray. "Heavenly Father, I come to you as humble as I know. Father, I want to thank you that you always hear me. Father, I come right now asking you to see about AJ who is the head of this house. Father, I pray right now that you touch him in a special way. I pray that you touch him from the top of his head to the bottom of his feet. Father, I pray that whatever hold the enemy has over him, you release him right now in the name of Jesus. I pray that you pick him up and build him up to become that man that you have called him to be. The father, the husband, the provider that you have called him to be. Father, I pray that whatever addictions he has, you will free him from that, from drugs and alcohol, to gambling. Take it all away, remove the taste for it, and make it so that it never comes back. Father, wherever Aaron is, I pray that he is safe and that he returns home. Touch Jamal as he lays in bed. Let them both know that we love and adore them and would do anything for them. Father, I pray that you will mend any brokenness inside of them and repair their relationship with their father. All these things I ask in your son Jesus's name, Amen."

"Thank you, Monica. No one has ever prayed for me like that. My parents rarely took us to church so the only time I really went was when my grandmother would take us, but the older she got, the less we would go. I would enjoy it, however I didn't understand a lot of it. Whenever the preacher was speaking, I always felt like he was talking over my head. Anyways, you should get going to the store before Jamal wakes up. Ok I'll see you later," AJ says before heading over to Jamal.

"Good morning Son. Come grab a seat, I have something I want to say to you…

I know I haven't been much of a father figure or any type of example to you and your brother and for that I'm sorry. I'm sorry for what happened with your brother. I wish I could take it all back. My father was never around and was addicted to drugs and alcohol. He was a gambler just like me and I swore I would not be like him if I ever had kids of my own and now, I see I'm just like him in more ways than I ever imagined. My father was a mean old dude and the older he got, the meaner he got. He used to beat us, something terrible. One time, he beat me so badly that I had to be rushed to the hospital and I remember my mother covering for him when the doctors asked her what happened to me. She told them that some neighborhood boys had jumped me. Both of my eyes were swollen shut, a broken nose and bruised liver. I think I was passing blood for weeks after that happened. That is why I stayed at the park and how I got so good at playing ball. I figured if I stayed out of the way and got good at basketball, he would have to be proud of me. Do you know my father never saw me play one game? NOT ONE, and I played all over this city. He wouldn't even help pay for the AAU teams that I played for. He thought basketball was a waste of time and money, so he wasn't going to spend his hard-earned money on any of it. So, when I got hurt in college, I remember him coming to the hospital and instead of him trying to console me and let me know things would be ok, he laughed at me and told me he knew that I wouldn't make it to the league, that it was just a matter of time. Soon after that, I was trying to get my knee together and he came home drunk and high and we got into it about the grass not being cut or something minor and he pushed me. I pushed him back and as he fell back, he hit his head on the edge of a table, and it did something to his spine and he ended up in a wheelchair until he passed. I have never forgiven myself for that and that's when I started drinking. Next thing I know, one thing lead to another. I was never the same after that, mentally, you know? To this day, I think that's what killed him. Being stuck in that wheelchair and not being able to move like he once did. That hurt me so bad to see him like that, knowing that I caused him to be in that chair," AJ says. Jamal takes it all in, then responds, "Pops, that wasn't your fault, you didn't mean for that to happen. You couldn't have known. Not to mention you didn't start that fight that day." "I know Son, but I still feel responsible for it all and it still haunts me," AJ replies.

Just then, Monica walks in and Jamal gets up to help grab the grocery bags she is carrying. "Baby, you need to get dressed for school. Get ready and I'll get you something to eat before you go," she says.

AJ then adds, "Son, do what you have to do tonight at the game, and I'll figure the rest out myself. I love you and I'm sorry that it took me so long to tell you." "It's cool Pops, I love you too," Jamal says.

GAME DAY

Jamal grabs his breakfast sandwich that Monica made for him and heads to school. Today is the big game and there is so much riding on this game. His mind is everywhere, and he is extremely nervous. Just as he gets to the end of the block, Big Nick and his crew roll up on him. "YO! Jamal come here, I need to holla at you for a minute," they say. "Naw man, I need to get to school, we got practice this morning and I can't be late," says Jamal. Big Nick screams at him, "BOY IF YOU DONT GET YO LITTLE ASS OVER HERE, YOU NOT GOING TO MAKE IT TO PRACTICE, SCHOOL OR NOWHERE ELSE!" Jamal makes his way closer to Nick and his goons. "Where is your brother? You two are always together," Big Nick says. "I don't know where he is. He didn't stay at the house last night. He should probably already be at school," Jamal says. "He better be and y'all better remember your lives and your parents' lives are depending on this game. Don't forget that! Now run along and get to school and don't be late," Big Nick says.

Jamal gets to the gym, and he can hear the sound of gym shoes screeching across the floor, which means he's late and Coach D is going to snap when he walks into the gym. Sure enough, as soon as Jamal shows his face, Coach D begins to snap, getting on him and the team about being late and not being mentally prepared. After practice, Jamal and Aaron begin to have words. "Man, where the hell have you been? We all have been worried sick about you," Jamal says to him. "Oh, you wasn't worried when Pops was about to smash me or when Big Nick and his guys were all up on me!" Aaron starts. "Bro, look I froze alright, what was I supposed to do with them, and they carry guns and all we had was a basketball and some old tennis shoes. As far as Pops goes, he didn't hit you, did he? Besides that, after you left, he went looking for you and something happened to him. I don't know what, but he looked like somebody beat him up pretty good. He also told me about him and his Pops and how he grew up. Now, I kind of understand why he is the way he is… Oh, and get this, for the first time ever, he told me he loved me and us! Can you believe that?" Jamal says. "Man get out of here with that soft shit. Pops don't love anybody but himself. He just told you all that BS because he was feeling bad and knew he was wrong. He was playing you just like he plays everybody. I don't believe nothing that dude got to say anymore," Aaron proclaims. Jamal adds, "Bro this time was different, he really meant it. If you would have been there, then you would understand," says Jamal.

"I don't care what you say, I don't believe any of it. I've heard him lie so many times and to so many people, Bro I know you can't trust anything he says. Besides, we have got other stuff to worry about tonight, so I need you to get your head in the game for tonight, can you do that Jamal?" Aaron says. "Yea I can do that and by the way… Big Nick stopped me on the way to school and gave me a reminder about tonight. He reminded me that if we don't pull this off, then he is going to kill all of us," Jamal says. "I'm already knowing, so get focused and keep your mouth shut. We got this and all that money is ours and we can stop living like bums. After this we can go to college, get a NIL deal and become rich. Ain't that what we have been talking about for years Jamal?" Aaron adds. Jamal nods, "Yea it is, but if anyone finds out about this, we could be in big trouble and then all of those dreams become nightmares. We could lose everything! Aaron, what if we went to the cops and told them what was going on, they would have to do something," Jamal says. "Bro, you know damn well what happens to snitches in our neighborhood. Besides, Big Nick got guys that work for the police. The minute they get word of this, we can cancel Christmas. We would be dead within the hour and so would Mom and Pops. Just go along with the plan and we will be cool, I promise," Aaron says. "I don't know Aaron, I'm nervous," Jamal says. "Don't be Bro, I got this," Aaron says with a wink. "Now let's get to class before either one of us can't play."

Back at the apartment, Monica and AJ are sitting at the table discussing if there is any way out of this mess and neither one of them has a viable solution. At this point, all they can do is pray and ask GOD for his protection. For the first time ever, Monica sees AJ vulnerable and not the cocky arrogant man she had grown to know. It was different seeing him this way. It is something that she had quietly longed for, but never thought she would ever see. It was as if she was seeing AJ for the first time. Even though the timing is terrible, she is glad to finally see it, hoping that this AJ will continue to stick around. As for the game tonight, they both understood the bind that they were in, so all they could do was let the game play out and pray that Aaron and Jamal could pull this off. "Babe, you look tired, why don't you go lay down and when you wake up, I'll fix you some lunch. I'll have to put it in the fridge, because I plan on working the noon to four shift so I can make the game tonight," Monica says. AJ replies, "Ok thank you. Monica, you know I love you, right?" "Yes, I know you do. Now get some rest and I'll see you at the game," she says.

As tradition, the school holds a pep rally the day of the big game. From serving the team breakfast to everyone gathering in the gym, to show their support for the team. It's a beautiful display of school pride shown by every student and faculty member. The principal gives a speech and then introduces the coach, who then gives his rah-rah speech. After that, he introduces all the players on the team, saving the stars for last and his two star players, Aaron and Jamal, who both take the microphone, give thanks to all who have supported them over these last four years. Aaron being Aaron, has them eating out of his hands. They are hanging onto every word that Aaron says. No one takes a seat the entire time he is talking. The hype is so great that Jamal doesn't have to say anything but 'Thank you for coming out'.

Its game time now and the gymnasium is filled to capacity. Everyone is at this game. From local politicians, celebrities, to the bagger at the local grocery store, as well as Big Nick and his guys sitting front row in the middle of the court. As Aaron and Jamal go through their warmups, they make eye contact with Big Nick, and they see him clapping for them and then he makes a money gesture, and from that, he makes a gun gesture as a subtle, but not so subtle reminder that they all had a lot riding on this game. Aaron taps Jamal on his chest and reminds him that they all have a lot to win or to lose on this game.

Just as the tip off begins, AJ and Monica walk into the gym and take their seat behind the team. It's the home team, the Crestwood Eagles vs the Hampton Lions. It's one of the oldest rivalries in the city and the gym is filled to capacity. It's standing room only.

Crestwood loses the tip and Hampton is off and running, pulling up from three and it's nothing but net. Jamal takes the ball out and passes it to Aaron. Aaron calls out the play and Jamal comes and sets the pick for him. Aaron takes two dribbles to his left, crosses back over to his right, and pulls a step back three and he hits nothing but net as well. The crowd goes crazy. There is so much electricity in the gym. For the entire first half, the two teams go back and forth. Crestwood would go up by one or two and then Hampton would go up by one or two. At the half, it's all tied up and Aaron has twenty-five while Jamal has twenty-two of the team's fifty-six points. When they come back out, AJ is standing at the door and wants to talk to both of them. Aaron looks at him with disgust and waives him off, while Jamal stays and talks with him. "What's up Pops?" Jamal asks. "Well Son, I noticed a few things about the kid you're guarding. He's pretty good, but I noticed every time he wants to shoot the ball, he always wants to get to his right. So, what he has been doing is he will start off like he wants to drive to his left and then he pulls the ball back so he can go to his right. If you jump him right when he does that, it's an easy steal for you if you time it right. Now when he does that, and you get the steal, have your brother leak out for the fast break and you will get some easy baskets and break this game wide open. Now they are tired already and their big man is in foul trouble; get him out the game and this will be a blowout by the fourth quarter," AJ says. "Ok Pops, I have to get back and warm up, thanks Pops. I'll let Aaron know." Jamal goes back and tells Aaron what AJ had to say, and Aaron is still so upset that he doesn't want to listen to anything AJ has to say. Crestwood gets the ball first and Aaron immediately goes to work and hits a wide open three to start the half as they head back on defense. Jamal's man gets the ball and just as AJ had told him, his guy starts off left and just as he is getting ready to pull back, Jamal jumps him and gets the steal just like AJ told him and he looks up and Aaron didn't take off like he was supposed to, so Jamal takes matters into his own hands and drives to the basket and finishes with a big dunk. The crowd goes nuts. They had seen this from Aaron, but never Jamal. The coach is yelling at them to get back, get back. The crowd is now yelling D-FENSE… D-FENSE! Jamal gets another steal, and this time Aaron does leak out and Jamal passes the ball to him and just like his pops, he finishes with a dunk and a wink at the crowd. AJ is sitting back quietly, but on the inside is bursting with pride and joy. The third quarter is now ending, and Crestwood now has a commanding lead, being up by twenty. Big Nick is getting a little nervous now and is glaring at Aaron and Jamal. He knows that this is about to get out of hand quickly with Hampton's best player and big man now fouled out of the game. As Jamal is shooting free-throws, Big Nick sends two of his guys over to sit next to AJ and Monica. Jamal sees this and gets nervous; he misses the first free-throw and then the second. He is extremely nervous and doesn't know what to do. Hampton rebounds the ball, pushes it up the court quickly and throws the ball up for an alley-oop. Aaron sees it coming and jumps up to grab the ball. He intercepts the ball and throws it to Jamal. Jamal gets the ball and begins to dribble up court. He looks over to see where Aaron is, and Aaron is pointing up meaning throw him the lob to get an easy dunk. It's something they have done a thousand times before from the concrete courts of the playground to every gym in the city. Jamal sets it up and throws the ball up so high, just when it looked like it was going to go out of bounds, Aaron jumps to grab it and he finishes with a thunderous dunk and hangs on the rim. Everyone in the gym is yelling and screaming at the play and no one notices that when Aaron comes down from the rim, how his knee buckles before he falls to the ground. Aaron is screaming in pain and slapping the floor. "Fuuuuuuuuccccckkkk," he screams, as he grabs his knee. The refs blow the whistle, and the coach and medical staff rush to his aid. Jamal is frozen at half court and AJ already knows what has happened, but doesn't want to believe it. The game is paused as they rush to get Aaron off the court. When the game resumes, it's Crestwoods possession and Jamal gets the ball, calls out a play and throws the ball away then he yells at his teammate for not being where he was supposed to be. It's obvious that Jamal is now shaken by what has happened. On Hampton's next possession, Jamal's man gets the ball and tries to use that same move on Jamal that he has been stealing it the entire second half; now Jamal tries to steal it and instead fouls him on the shot, and he makes it, creating a three-point opportunity. He sinks the free-throw and now the game is getting close again, but without Aaron, things are getting tougher. Crestwood's coach calls a time out and takes Jamal out the game. It's clear to him that Jamal's head is no longer in the game. Jamal heads down to the end of the bench and begins to talk with Aaron. "Bro, what's going on, what are they saying about your situation?" "I'm not sure Bro, they think it might be some ligament damage or a tear. We won't know until I get some x-rays later tonight, but for now you need to get your head out your ass and get back out there; you know what we got riding on this. Get back in the game and do what you do. We need to win this game by no more than nine. We are only down by one and that's nothing, we got three minutes to pull this off. I need you to go back out there and pretend it's just me and you playing one on one. Nobody out there can stop you Bro. You got this and remember you're the best out there since I'm not there," Aaron says. Jamal nods, then turns to the coach, "Coach, I'm ready to go back in." "Are you sure Jamal?" "Yes, Coach, I'm sure. I got this." "Then get back in there and show me what you got." Jamal gets back on the court and the crowd roars, as he starts going crazy. He can't miss; everything he throws up is now going in. Crestwood goes up by nine and there is thirty seconds left and they have the ball. All Jamal has to do now is just stall and not score another point. Hampton goes to double-team Jamal and Jamal passes the ball. His teammate shoots the three and it seemed like the ball was in the air for an eternity. When it hits the rim, it rolls around and around and finally falls through the net. Crestwood is up by eleven with just eight seconds left. Jamal's heart just sank into his socks; he knows what this means. If he had just held the ball, he could have shot free-throws and missed them. Hampton takes the ball out and the coach is yelling 'not to foul'. Jamal knows that they will probably just dribble the time out and not attempt to shoot the ball. As soon as Hampton throws the ball in, Jamal goes after it and fouls the guy by going after the ball. Hampton now gets to shoot two free-throws. The coach is furious at Jamal and is screaming at him from the sidelines. The refs gets the shooter to the line and first one goes in nothing but net. Jamal begins to think that maybe they now have a chance. All this guy has to do is make this one and they're home free with nothing else to worry about. They will get to keep all the money, no one will be hurt and Big Nick will be out of their lives forever. Jamal has never prayed so hard in his life. The ref gets the ball out of the net and instructs everyone that Hampton has one more shot. He hands the guy the ball and he takes two dribbles, takes a deep breath, dribbles two more times. He then spins the ball, pauses, bends his knees and finally shoots the ball. It spins end over end with perfect rotation and it hits the front on the rim and bounces back to the backboard, hit the front of the rim again and finally spins around the rim and finally drops through the net. Jamal is so relieved that he takes a deep sigh of relief. Now all they have to do is throw the ball in and this game is over back to a nine-point lead. As soon as the buzzer goes off, the crowd rushes the floor. The players lift Jamal into the air and the crowd is chanting his name. Reporters are coming from everywhere, wanting to talk to Jamal. For the first time in his life, Jamal feels like he is important, like he matters and he is not in Aaron's shadow any longer. Then reality hits him, that Aaron is about to be taken to the hospital and he needs to be there. "Jamal, Jamal, come here, there is somebody that wants to meet you," the coach says. "Coach, I really want to go check on Aaron." "I know Son, but this recruiter has traveled a long way to see you and your brother, and he is looking forward to meeting you," Coach says. "Hello Mr. Rose… Jamal, right?" the recruiter says. "Yes Sir. My name is Coach Travis and I'm the recruiter for 'U of I'. I was wondering if I could schedule a sit-down meeting with you, your brother and your parents and then maybe a trip out to 'U of I' for all of you to see our campus and see what we have to offer both of you. I think we would be a good fit for you and vice versa. I understand you want to get to the hospital to be with your brother, so here is my card. Call me any time day or night. Tell Aaron, we send our regards and that we are praying for a speedy recovery," the recruiter says. "Thank you Coach… I, well we, appreciate that, and we will be in touch."

Jamal leaves the school and rushes over to the hospital. He is a nervous wreck and all he can do is think the worst and reflect back on Pop's injury.

"Mom, Pops, what's going on with Aaron? How is Aaron's knee? Will he be able to play next week?" His dad replies, "Jamal calm down. Your brother is getting his knee looked at right now."

The doctor arrives and begins, "Hello Aaron, Mr. and Mrs. Rose, my name is Dr. Craig, I just finished looking at Aaron's x-rays and right now there is so much swelling around his knee that it's hard to tell just how much damage was done. For right now though, I would suggest he stay off of it the next few weeks until the swelling goes down. We can schedule an appointment about two weeks out and look at it again and then go from there. He should ice it a couple times a day and stay off of it as much as possible. If he has any problems or if he has any more pain, please give me a call. The nurse will be in shortly with detailed instructions. Do you guys have any questions?" Aaron heard every word and interjects, "Doc, are you telling me I can't play ball anymore for the next two weeks?" "Yes Aaron, no more basketball, at least for the next two weeks." Aaron presses, "Doc, we got games, and I can't miss them, my team needs me! Not to mention we will be playing the state tournament soon and I have to be ready. You got to get me right DOC!"

"Aaron, I can't promise you anything. We have to wait until the swelling goes down before we can do anything. In the meantime, you have to stay off of it and you have to make sure you are icing it on a regular basis," the doctor adds.

AJ chimes in, "Don't worry Aaron, we will get through this!" "What do you mean we?" Aaron rebuts, "You ain't never there, and last time I checked, you was going in on me remember?" "Aaron, about that, I'm sorry and I want to explain that whole situation," AJ tearfully exclaims. Aaron cut him off, "Man, I ain't trying to hear nothing you got to say right now. I don't even know why you're here. You must want some money or something? You haven't seen us play all summer or since the season started and now that I'm down, you want to see how your meal ticket is doing. Man miss me with all that. I just want to get dressed and get up out of here," Aaron says. "Aaron Rose, you can't talk to your father like that. He is still your father, and you will respect him as such," Monica jumps in. "Ma, why you standing up for him after everything he has done to all of us? Not to mention what he just did to me. He was about to snatch me up and punch me. Did you know that?" "Yes, Aaron, I heard all about it and yes it wasn't the best way to handle it, but we can talk about all of that later. Let's get you out of here and back to the house so you can put your leg up and rest," Monica says. "No Ma, we can get out of here, but I'm not going back to the house with him. I got me a spot and I'm cool there." "Aaron, that is not your home and you're still our responsibility." "Mom no disrespect, but Jamal and I been taking care of ourselves, you're always at work and Pops ain't never there. I got a roof over my head and food to eat. I'm good. Y'all just worry about Jamal," Aaron explains. AJ turns to Monica and says, "Babe, let it go. He's upset and just needs some time to cool off." "No, AJ, this my baby and he needs to be with me, with us!" Aaron replies, "Mom, I'm not coming back to the house. I like it on my own and I'm cool. Can we just please move on from this? Mom, I'm not trying to hurt you or your feelings, none of that, but you left when you were what, fifteen, so what's the difference?" I'm two years older than you were when you left." "Son, my situation is different from your situation," Monica says. "Mom, just know that I love you, but I'm not coming back home," Aaron repeats. Monica begins to weep heavily and runs out the room. Jamal sees her and runs into the room thinking the worst has happened. "Pops, Aaron, what's going on? Why did mom run out crying? You cool bro?" AJ replies, "Everything is fine,

Son. Aaron is going to be fine. Your mom is crying because your brother isn't coming home with us, and your mom got upset." Jamal turns to Aaron, "Bro, why are you not coming back home? Come on Bro, y'all need to squash that! Tell him Pops, everything going to be like it was." Aaron replies, "Jamal, I don't care what he says, I'm not coming back. I don't want to go back to living like that anymore. I'm cool where I'm at and I like being on my own." Jamal's eyes begin to tear up and the nurse walks in with the discharge papers. Jamal leaves the room and goes to look for his mother. AJ signs the papers while Aaron begins to get dressed. AJ takes a deep breath and says, "Aaron look, let me just say this to you before you leave. I know I have made a lot of mistakes over the years. I haven't been the best to your mother or you boys. I can admit that now. I take full responsibility for all my actions; however, I love all of you. I never had a father, so I didn't know how to be one. My father was never there and when he was there, he beat me. He beat me so badly that one time I had to go to the hospital. I didn't want that for you boys, and I was trying to capture something that wasn't there. When I hurt my knee, it took so much from me. I felt like I had lost everything, and I didn't know how to deal with it. I have never lost at anything in my life. Then when your mom had you and your brother, I didn't have anything, so everything just seemed to be hitting me at once. I knew I had to do something, so I started hustling even harder and one thing led to another. I started drinking more to cope with everything and next thing you know, I was willing to do just about anything to keep things going. The more I thought I was catching up, the more things got out of hand. I was no longer the center of attention, I was just a nobody and that's a hard pill to swallow. Tonight, watching you on that court reminded me so much of myself; it was as if I had traveled back in time and was watching myself on the court. Both of you are really good, but the way you play, you remind me so much of me.

Then to see you wink at the crowd and they go nuts like they did, that was truly a flashback for me." Aaron responds, "Why are you telling me all this?" AJ replies, "I just wanted you to understand some of why I am the way I am. It was never that I didn't love you guys. I just didn't know how to love you! I never saw how a man is supposed to treat his wife or his family. The lessons I got from my dad, I wouldn't want my worst enemies to have to go through what I went through." AJ eyes begin tearing up as he pours his heart out to Aaron. "All I can say is, I'm sorry. I'm not using this as an excuse or anything like that, I just wanted you to know why I am the way that I am. I pray one day you can forgive me." "I'm sorry that you had to go through that Pops, but today ain't the day. Maybe before you had snatched me up, maybe I would have understood, but when you did that, it showed me what you think of me. You would do me like you would an average Joe on the street. That showed me what you think of me. All these years you have never been there, so when I went out and made something happen for all of us, not just for me…not for Jamal, for all of us... I knew we could do it. I told y'all this was going to be a great come up for all of us. Now look, we all can eat good until we get into college and get NIL deals. As for right now, my ride is here, so I'm going to take off. That money that I left there, y'all can just keep that. I got enough stashed away to keep me for the rest of this year. Let Mom and Jamal know I'll be cool and I'll see him back at school on Monday." AJ holds his arms like he's trying to give him a hug and Aaron sidesteps him as he walks past him on crutches. AJ is trying his best to keep from showing how hurt he is, so he stays in the room for a minute, trying to keep his composure.

Monica and Jamal walk back into the room and see AJ standing there with tears in his eyes, and for the first time in their lives, they began to see him differently. He's not that mean, uncaring, unloving, selfish man. In that very moment, they could see a hurt father, a sensitive loving, caring man who really does care about his family. "He's gone, I drove my son away just like my father did. I can't believe I drove him away. I'm so sorry, I'm so sorry!" AJ says as he sobs and Monica moves in to hold him as he begins weeping heavily. "…I'm sorry, I'm sorry!" Jamal moves in to hug AJ as well. He grabs Jamal and squeezes him tight. Please forgive me Son. I really wanted to do better for you boys, I wanted to give you more than what I had. I wanted to be better than my father was to me, and I failed you all. I'm so sorry." "It's ok Pops, we forgive you. Aaron will forgive you too, just give him some time and he will come around. Aaron is just hurt right now between what happened with the two of you and him getting hurt and not being able to play; his mind is all over the place. You know how he gets when he can't have his way. He will pout for a few days and then be back like nothing happened. Just wait and see. Watch what I tell you," Jamal says. "Yea Ok Son, we will give him a few days and some space. Thank you, Son. I love you; I love both of y'all and I promise things will be better. I will be better and do better for myself and for y'all."

GETTING RECRUITED

few weeks have gone by, and Jamal has been playing lights out. Every gym he plays at, there are tons of reporters and recruiters there trying to get a piece of him. He's often embarrassed by the amount of attention he's now getting. He is so used to Aaron getting it all and him playing second fiddle. Aaron is still in recovery so all he can do is sit on the sidelines and give pointers. The swelling in his knee has gone down and it turned out to be just a strain. Once he can get through a full practice session with no swelling and pain he will be allowed to play again. It's hard for him not being out there or being the center of attention. He is still getting some looks, but nothing solid until the recruiters can see him back on the court. His relationship with Jamal is still strained and his relationship with AJ is still nonexistent. Recently, AJ hasn't missed a game or a beat when it comes to being a father figure and with his relationship with Monica and Jamal. He is more tentative, loving and intentional with his actions. It's only been a short time, but every day, things move in the right direction. They even went to church together as a family. It was the first time they had been in a church that Jamal could remember. Everything seemed to be getting better in their lives. With the money they got from Big Nick, they even found a nice apartment to live in. It has three rooms so Aaron and Jamal wouldn't have to share anymore if Aaron comes back. It is a major upgrade from that run down little apartment they had before. Every room is fully furnished, and the fridge and cupboards remain fully stocked. The only thing that is missing is Aaron. The more things seem to be getting better at home, the more distant Aaron seems to be. It is as if he hates them for doing better and all the attention Jamal is getting.

It's now been about a month and a half and Aaron is ready to get back on the court. It is his first game back, and he is initially a little timid. You can tell that he isn't sure of how well he has healed. Where he would have normally went in for a dunk, he is settling for the layup with no flair at all. Not only does he not trust his knee, it seems as if he doesn't trust Jamal either. Instead of passing the ball to him for an easy basket, he would take a difficult shot or just look off Jamal all together and pass the ball to another player. Every time Jamal would ask him about it, he would simply say, "My bad Bro, I didn't see you" or "My fault, I thought you were going to cut this way or that way" As long as they were winning, coach didn't have anything to say. As the current game progresses Jamal figures that since Aaron won't pass him the ball, he would just have to do other things to score and to stand out. Any time the ball would come off the backboard, Jamal would grab it. Whenever the man he was guarding gets the ball, Jamal would find a way to steal the ball and either get a layup or get the assist. Either way, Jamal is commanding the game without doing all the scoring. At the end of the game, Aaron finishes with thirty points, but Jamal ends up with eight-teen points, fifteen rebounds and ten assists, a triple double. It isn't flashy at all, but he is very effective. Once again, the crowd rushes the floor and there are reporters everywhere shoving cameras in their faces. Aaron, Jamal, how do you both feel about tonight's game. "I think it was a good warm up game to get us back in sync. I felt a little rusty at first since this was my first game back since I hurt my knee, but I still think I did pretty good, I mean I did get thirty tonight. I'm just saying," Aaron says. "Jamal, what about you? How do you think tonight's game went?" "I think tonight's game went just the way coach said it would. It was a great team win and it was good to have Aaron back with us again. He's our leader and we kind of just play off of him and his energy," Jamal explains. "Well, the last couple of weeks you had been that leader. Was it hard for you to take a back seat to your brother?" a reported says. "I don't think I took a backseat at all. It's just that my role has changed with Aaron being back. For me, as long as we get the win, that's all that matters to me," Jamal explains. "One last question for both of you. It looks like you guys could possibly be matched up with Hampton again for the state title game. What are your feelings about the possible rematch?" One reporter asks. "Well last time, I didn't play the full game, and they made it close. This next time, it won't be so close!" Aaron says. "What about you Jamal?" The reporter asks. "Well, all we can do is play our game and not worry about the things we can't control. I'm sure they will be prepared just like we will, so we will see. I think it will be a good game," Jamal humbly replies, before turning to his brother, "Aaron, coach wants us to come back for the team meeting." Jamal takes off and Aaron slowly makes his way back, signing autographs and shaking hands.

He misses the attention from everyone. On the way back to the locker room, AJ is standing by the locker room doors and tries to congratulate Aaron as he walks by. "Good game Son," AJ says with pride. Aaron acknowledges him with just a head nod and continues to walk into the locker room. It's hurtful, but AJ understands that it's going to take some time for Aaron to get past what happened. It's a new day for all of them.

It's obvious that something is bothering Jamal by the way he's throwing his clothes around and slamming doors. "Hey, hey what's wrong with you? What's going on?" AJ asks Jamal. "I'm sick of Aaron being such a spoiled brat. Everything is all about him and what he wants. He has to be the one that gets all the shine. He has to be the one that has to be out front. Did you notice how he didn't pass me the ball tonight? I was wide open, and he just looked me off or just threw up a shot. He just didn't want me to shine. When he was out, we played like a team. Everybody was on the same page and now it's all about him. When he was talking to the reporters, he didn't even mention the team or me and I'm tired of feeling like I'm not in the room when he is around, like I'm a second thought. Pops I'm just as good if not better, but no one sees that because I'm always playing second fiddle to him. It's almost as if he thinks I'm his shadow or something. People only see me because of the light that is cast upon him." AJ thinks before responding, "Son, first of all, calm down. Both of you have a lot of talent. You may not have had thirty tonight, but you played your ass off. You had a triple double. You played an all-around great game! Look, scouts want more than just someone who can score. They are looking for all around talent. As far as you being in his shadow, part of that is your two personalities. He has always been the outspoken one, and you have always been the quiet one. I thought you didn't care about any of that. Ever since I can remember, you have always wanted to go to college to be a lawyer or doctor first and basketball was second. Has that changed?" AJ says. Jamal replies, "No!!! I mean, I don't know. It's just that these past couple of weeks everything seemed like it was going great, and people were noticing me, Jamal Rose, for what seemed like the first time ever, and I guess I got caught up in it all." His father then says, "So, let me ask you this, are you really mad at Aaron or are you mad that you didn't get the attention that you had been getting?" "I don't know, Pops I mean it was nice to get some attention for once and not just to be known as Aaron's twin or just twin. People got to see Jamal and I did like it! I have to admit, Jamal says" "Son, there is nothing wrong with that. Everybody wants to be seen and celebrated for their wins. I think you just have to learn how to find yourself and your voice and still be Jamal. Now what I saw out there tonight was incredible. I saw a great all-around game. You both complement each other. Thanks, Pops, I needed to hear that. Wait you remembered that I want to be a doctor or lawyer? I haven't talked about that in a long time." AJ smiles, "Of course, I remember Son, I know I had been absent a lot; however, I want you to know that I have always loved you boys and I have always been so proud of you guys. I would brag about you and your brother to all the guys. I even watched you guys on the court from time to time. I didn't want to be that dad who was always yelling in the stands about the refs or the coaches, yelling at you guys if you missed a layup or didn't get back on defense. I had seen enough and heard enough of that for a lifetime, and I didn't want you guys to go through that. I wanted you to fall in love with the game just like I did - on your own and not because I played. I didn't want you to end up like me, and it hurts to say that. I mean every father wants their son to be like a little mini me and I had done so many things wrong. You two are the only things that I can say I didn't screw up or so I thought, that if I kept my distance, then I wouldn't screw you guys up. Now I see I couldn't have been more wrong. I should have been there, now Aaron hates me even more," AJ says. Jamal turns and says, "He doesn't hate you Pops, he is just hurt, that's all and for the record, I don't hate you either. In fact, I think you're pretty cool. Not many kids can say their Pops is a legend. "Thank you, Son. I appreciate it, I really do!" The two embrace one another. AJ then adds, "Oh, by the way, guess who just got a job working first shift and making some good money, and check this out, I'll be getting a company car!" Jamal beams with pride, "Pops that's what's up… CONGRATULATIONS!" "Thanks Son. Now your mom can quit taking all those shifts and find something that she wants to do on her own terms," AJ says. "Have you told her yet? No, I just found out myself while we were at the game, and I didn't want to interfere with your big win. One game away from going to state."

AJ continues, "Jamal, let me ask you something. After we left church a couple of weeks ago, I started going through a pamphlet they gave us, and I saw where they did family counseling. I was wondering if you would be open to going with your mother and me. No pressure, and if you don't want to go, I understand. We have been through so much and I was hoping this could heal our family and get us back on track." "I'm not sure Pops. Sitting down and telling some stranger about everything we have been through, I just don't see how that is going to help us," Jamal says. "I don't know either Son. I guess we can find out more about it when we go back on Sunday. I was just curious if you would even want to go. I know your mom would love it," AJ tells Jamal.

On the other side of town, Aaron is out with his new crew of friends. They are smoking, drinking and hanging out on the corner, when Big Nick rolls up on Aaron and his guys. "What up my boy? Great game, I see you went off and got thirty on them.

Congratulations!" Big Nick says. "Thanks, Big Nick, yea it was just a little something. I should have had more if a couple of my threes would have fell instead of rimming out," Aaron says. "Yea I saw that, well here you go my boy, a little something to show you my appreciation from that other situation." Nick hands AJ a roll of hundreds all rolled up with a rubber band around them. "That's all you too my man. Get you and that pretty lil' girl I saw you all hugged up with something nice. You know women love to be taken care of. They don't like their men being broke and no ends in their pockets." Aaron replies, "Yea I feel you, thank you man. You know it wouldn't have been that close if I hadn't hurt my knee." "I know young blood. All that matters is the "W" right. So, listen, I was thinking and looking at your schedule and if you win this next game, you could possibly be matched with Hampton again for the state championship. I was thinking maybe we can run that back again with that bet. If that happens, we just need to make sure we cover the spread," Big Nick suggests once again. Aaron replies, "I don't know Nick. The first time, Jamal was on board. Now, we are not even speaking and I'm not sure. This time, it's just me," Aaron says. "Maybe I didn't make myself clear. If Crestwood plays Hampton for the CHIP, we will be running that same bet! That money I just handed you, that you so graciously accepted, was an advance on our business deal. So, like I said, go out and enjoy it with your girl and have fun. Relax, you got this with or without Jamal's help. I would suggest that whatever you two got going on, you better fix it and make sure y'all on the same page for your sake. Remember you just took my money, and I don't play when it comes to my money. Have a good night!"

Aaron's whole demeanor and attitude has now changed. He is visibly angry and shook by this conversation with Big Nick to the point that he gets into a shoving match with one of his guys for no reason. The crew breaks it up and Aaron storms off walking. The gravity of the situation he just put himself and his family in once again is now weighing heavy on his mind. He knows he is not one hundred percent, and neither is his relationship with Jamal. Hampton hasn't been playing that well since their game; they have barely beaten the same teams that Crestwood has been blowing out. The way Aaron sees it, the spread will be bigger than the nine that it was before. It will probably be like fifteen or more, which will be harder for them. Aaron knows he has to get Jamal on board or at least get him to trust him on the court.

DIVINE INTERVENTION

It's Sunday morning and AJ wakes up a little earlier than usual. Something is different about today and he is excited to get to church. He's so excited that he even wants to go to Sunday School. When they get to the church, he is greeted by Sister Fricks and the other students in the class. "In today's lesson, we will discuss a very important story in the bible that gives us life lessons even in today's world. It's the story of "The Prodigal Son." In this story, I would like to highlight three things as it relates to us today. Those things are repentance, forgiveness and redemption," the teacher says. AJ quietly sits in his seat as this story is starting to hit home with him. He begins to reflect on his own life as he learns more about the story. The first lesson he picks up on is repentance.

It's been 2 months since he did any type of drugs or had any alcohol and now he can see things clearly. For the first time in two months, he has a clear mind, and he is sorry for the way he has acted. As the story progresses, the young son has now squandered all he had and now has to come back to his father. AJ could see himself as it related to coming back to church and his Heavenly Father and how he was received with open arms. He could see how since his return to church, his life has seemed to turn for the better. The second part of the lesson is probably the hardest for AJ. It is about forgiveness. His eyes begin to water as the teacher explains that if he wanted to be forgiven, he must learn to forgive as well; not only his father, but himself. Mrs. Fricks says something that was so profound to him. She states that "forgiveness is not for the other person, it's for you!" She goes on to say, "Forgiveness frees you from carrying an unnecessary weight that we tend to carry and if we want GOD to forgive us, we must forgive others. Even though his father is no longer living, it is still necessary for AJ to forgive him and let the past go so he can move on. The third and final part of this story is about redemption. This is something that has been weighing heavily on AJ's mind. He is finally ready to give his life over to Christ to atone for his sins. Everything seems to be falling into place for AJ and his family. Now if only Aaron would come home, this would make everything complete.

All that morning forgiveness kept replaying in his head from how his father was with him to how he was with Aaron and Jamal. His father may have scarred him physically, but he has scared his boys emotionally. That is a tough pill for AJ to swallow. He never wanted to be like his father and yet somehow, he made similar mistakes. At the end, AJ is feeling like the weight of the world is slowly being lifted from his shoulders, and much better than when they arrived. As they are transitioning from Sunday School into the worship service. His thoughts start to shift towards Aaron and what he must be going through and feeling. All these years of not being there for Aaron and Jamal, not showing up for games or providing for them like other fathers do for their children. *He must really hate me. Then for me to almost put my hands on him. How can he ever forgive me? Will it take fifty-some odd years for him to forgive me like it did for me to forgive my Pops? God I hope not!* As AJ's thoughts run wild, he hears Pastor Chris say, "If there is anyone who would like to be baptized, now is the time to come forward. AJ looks around to see if anyone else is moving towards the front. No one is coming and yet he is moving in what seemed like slow motion to the front. There is a pulling in him to get baptized, to go under the water and become new. He had tried everything else from drinking, smoking and being out in the streets and nothing ever made him feel like this. Nothing ever felt so right. AJ knew this was the right decision for him and his family. As he walked towards the front of the church, right behind him came Monica and then Jamal. Both were following his lead. This was a proud moment for AJ; he was finally leading his family in the right direction. The church secretary came down to get their names and info. After announcing them and welcoming them to the church, Pastor Chris begins to talk to them about how great a decision the three of them had just made and how impactful seeing the three of them would be for others. What AJ didn't realize was that by coming and giving his life over to the Lord, he was breaking generational curses.

At the end of the service, it is customary for the congregation to walk around and greet the new members, as well as to welcome them to the church. After everyone had come around, one gentleman comes back to talk to AJ, Monica and Jamal. "Hello and welcome to the church, are you the same AJ Rose who used to hoop back in the day over on the South Side?" "Yea, that was me, how can I help you?" AJ said. "Man, me, and my best friend Troy Brooks used to play against you. We went to Hampton. We always wondered what happened to the legend." AJ takes a good look at him, "Wait a minute, you're Terrance Mays? The hooper and basketball star? I remember you as well! How you been?" Terrance smiles and says, "I've been good man. So, this is one of your sons following in your footsteps? I read about the triple double you had in your last game." "Hello Sir, and yes that was me. My name is Jamal. It's nice to meet you." AJ then adds, "I'm sorry, Terrance this is my girl and his mother, Monica." "Hello, nice to meet you," Monica says. "It's nice to meet you as well." AJ, curious – asks, "So, Terrance what happened to you and Troy after high school?" "Well, the short story is that we both went off to college and then became lawyers. Now we have our own practice," Terrance says. "Wait, Brooks and Mays is you and Troy? You guys had that murder trial with the Senator right?" "Yes that was us." "Man, you guys are doing it. I've seen your commercials and billboards all over town," AJ adds. "We doing ok. Well, I don't want to hold you guys up. I just wanted to come speak and see if it was truly the legend AJ Rose. You guys have made a great choice choosing this church. Pastor Chris is great, and the congregation is truly the bomb. They are so loving and nice. It's like everyone here is family. We have a saying that you may come here as a friend, but you will leave as family," Terrance adds. "Yea we felt that when we first got here and now even more so," AJ replies. "Well, it was good to see you AJ and I hope to see more of you all. If you ever need anything, here is my number, just give me a call," Terrance offers. "OK cool, maybe we can get together and hang out sometime and reminisce and talk about old times with Troy." "I would love it too." Then they all wave goodbye to Terrance. On the way to the car AJ begins to think about his time in high school and now his boys only need one more game and they will be heading to the state finals. It's incredible to see how everyone in the town is excited to watch their games. Aaron and Jamal have been on every news outlet on TV and in the newspaper. They are like rock stars. Everywhere they go, they are mobbed by fans and reporters to sign autographs or give interviews. Arron thrives on it and Jamal doesn't care for it. He still feels like the shadow and that nobody really sees him for who he is outside of basketball and being Aaron's twin. It doesn't matter what else he does outside of playing basketball, he still seems invisible.

Now at school, Aaron sees Jamal walking in the hallway in-between classes. "Jamal, Jamal, JAMAL, I know you hear me!" Aaron shouts. "What Bro?" Jamal yells back. "Look, I know you and I have not been seeing eye-to-eye lately, but we have to talk about this game Bro. One-night Big Nick and his guys cornered me at my girl's crib and held me at gunpoint. He told me that if I wanted to live another second, we had to fix this game too. Bro, I had no choice. He was playing Russian Roulette with me. He would spin the chamber just like they do in the movies and then pull the trigger. I had no choice but to agree to do it.

I need to know if you are on board with me or not bro. You know what will happen if Big Nick doesn't get what he wants from us." Jamal turns to him and says, "Aaron, I told you the last time, I didn't want to have anything to do with that." "Yea OK, I see you and Pop didn't mind spending that money that I left. Y'all in a new crib, you wearing those new J's, I bet you eating good too right? Yea that's what I thought. Look if we don't pull this off, you know Big Nick and his goons will be coming to see all of us and not in a good way. So, whether you want to or not, all our lives are in danger, and we need to get it together," Aaron says while pointing his finger in Jamal's chest. "Fine! I'll do it. I'll help you this one last time, but just know this will be the last time and the last time we play together," Jamal says. "Bro you bugging. Let's just get through these last few games and we can talk about this later," Aaron says. "Yea whatever, I have to get to class," Jamal says. "You are still just going to turn your back on me huh? After all I have done for you. How I stood up for you even when you were too scared to stick up for yourself. Bro I have been there our whole life protecting you and helping you out and you can't do this one thing for me, for Mom and Pops? That's tragic Bro! For real, for real!" Jamal rebuts, "Aaron you act like I ain't never done nothing for you. Yea, you have always taken care of me, but I've always had your back too. Remember when Pops told you to clean the house and you wanted to go play ball. I stayed home and cleaned up for you so he wouldn't break you off, what about that time when you didn't want to be bothered with that one girl so I took her out for you so you could be with Michelle. Aaron, I have always had your back. Whatever you needed, I have always done what you wanted. You can't say that I haven't. So, I'm not trying to hear any of that. As for the game, I will help you only because of Mom and Pops. I don't want anything to happen to them. Look tonight let's just take care of this game against West and then we will talk about Hampton and if you look me off one more time it's going to be a problem," Jamal says. "Look Jamal, you can drop that tough guy routine. We both know you are not going to do anything so quit fronting!" Aaron says.

It's game time; Aaron and Jamal are on fire, they can't miss. Everything they throw up is going in. They are playing as if their very lives depend on this game. It's almost as if the other team is playing in slow motion. Both Aaron and Jamal have twenty-five at the half and they're up thirty holding the other team to just twenty points. As they head into the locker room, the crowd is hyped, and so is the team. Everyone is high fiving each other and dancing. The atmosphere is electric. Aaron and Jamal are standing in the middle of the locker room nose to nose. "Now that's how we play Jamal. They can't stop us Bro! I told you they can't stop us. All we have to do is just keep balling like this and we will win state, I promise you!" Aaron says. "Yes Sirrrr. Let's Goooooooooooo!" Jamal screams out. The two of them are so in sync. That twin intuition is in full effect. They start off the third quarter just like they ended the second quarter, throwing down thunderous dunks and raining three pointers. By the end of the quarter, both Aaron and Jamal are sitting on the sidelines and cheering on the other players that don't get to play much. This game is all but over. It's official, Crestwood vs Hampton rematch for the State Championship game. As the time ticks off the clock, the fans rush the floor and place Aaron and Jamal on their shoulders. The announcers try desperately to get the crowd off of the floor so they can have the trophy presentation. After a couple of announcements, the crowd slowly rescinds back to the stands. Aaron and Jamal walk towards the podium to receive their team trophy. The two carry the trophy back to the team where everyone is jumping around and dancing. Aaron calls the team together so they can all get a chance to hold the trophy.

"Great game Bro, man you was balling!" Aaron tells Jamal. "Yea it felt like old times playing with you again." "If we play like this when we play Hampton, we gone kill them. They won't stand a chance against us," Aaron tells Jamal. "Look, let's just enjoy this win right now and worry about Hampton tomorrow. Bro we are going down state and playing for a state title… AAAYYYYYY LET'S GO!" Jamal screams out.

As the two walk out together laughing and signing autographs, Monica and AJ are standing outside the locker room entrance.

Monica reaches out to embrace both boys and expresses how proud she is of them. AJ moves in to share his congratulations as well and Aaron once again pushes him away. It hurts him to his core; however, he knows that this was of his own doing and that it would take time to heal, so he backs off and goes to greet Jamal next. "Hey man, great game out there. You guys looked good out there working together. Chemistry really shows when you both work together." "Yea Pops, that was probably one of the best games Aaron and I have ever played together," Jamal says. "Well, I hope you guys saved a little bit for that state title game," AJ says. "I know right. Man, this is crazy, we actually have a chance to win state." "Yes you do Son. Now get changed, we are going out to celebrate. Tell Aaron we want him to come too. He will probably turn us down, but at least we asked. I don't want him thinking that we don't want him around. If he says no, then that's fine. I don't want to ruin this night for either of you, so don't you get upset either. Just let it go, ok?" AJ asks. "Ok Pops, I'll ask him," Jamal replies.

As AJ and Monica are walking out of the arena and waiting for Jamal to come out, AJ sees Big Nick harassing Aaron outside the arena away from the rest of the team. AJ runs over to them and steps between the two. "Ay, what you doing? Let my son go!" Big Nick responds, "Who the hell do you think you talking to AJ!?" One of Nick's guys punches AJ in the stomach and AJ drops to his knees. That's for thinking you run something out here. You may have been the man back in the day on the court, but out here, I'm the man and it's what I say goes. I say who scores, who passes the rocks, who lives and who dies, and tonight is your lucky night. Since your boys just got us to the state title game, I'm going to let you live. Don't you ever think that you can step to me again though… Next time I won't be so nice. Lil Dude you know what I told you. I got money on you boys to win and cover the spread, so it would be in your best interest and in your family's best interest to make sure that happens. If that don't happen, people will be throwing roses on the concrete court in your memories."

"Uhm excuse me, AJ is everything all right over here?" Terrance walks up and asks. "Yea we good Terrance." "Man, who the fuck is this square ass dude all up in our business?" Big Nick says. "My name is Terrance Mays. Who are you?" "I'm none of your business." Nick's guys start to walk up on Terrance and AJ comes to his defense. "Ay y'all hold up, hold up. Terrance is an old friend of mine and was just coming to meet Aaron. He was a big time hooper and baseball player back in the day." "Ok, ok I think I remember you. Now you're a big-time lawyer right?" Big Nick asks. "Yes I'm an attorney," Terrance responds. "Ok well let me get your card. I might need your services one day." Terrance reluctantly gives him a card and starts to walk away with Aaron and AJ. As they get to a safe distance, A J stops them and thanks Terrance for stepping in. "What was that all about AJ?" Terrance asks. "It was nothing T, he was just an overly upset fan trying to get to Aaron that's all." Terrance interjects, "Man, I know who Big Nick is and what he is all about. I know he is not just upset about the game." "It's cool T, trust me. We are good," AJ says. "OK AJ, but if you need me, just call. I know guys like him and before you know it, they will have you caught up in some mess," Terrance says. "We good Terrance I promise. Anyway, this is my other son, Aaron." "Man, you guys look exactly alike," Terrance says surprised. "Yes Sir, we hear that a lot," Aaron says. "Well, great game tonight. I was telling your dad and your brother at the last game you two are amazing. I haven't seen anyone play like that since your dad." "Thank you. Yea we learned a lot from him," Aaron says. "Well, I'm not going to hold you guys up, but if you need anything at all, please don't hesitate to call me. Again, great game Aaron and I'll be at the game cheering you guys on," Terrance says. "Thank you Sir, I appreciate it," Aaron replies as Terrance walks away.

"Aaron, what was that all about this time?" AJ asks. "You know how Big Nick is Pops. He wants us to throw another game so he can win some money and if we don't do it, he said he would kill all of us again. I don't know what we gone do Pops; he has been following me around town. Everywhere I go, either he or his guys are there. I can't shake them. Why can't I just play ball like other kids Pops? Why can't I just live a normal life like everybody else? All I want to do is play ball." Tears begin flowing. He grabs on to AJ and holds him tight. "I know Son and unfortunately, a lot of that is my fault and how I raised you boys. I tried so hard not to be like my father, but that's exactly who I turned into. I'm sorry son that I raised my hand to you like I did and I'm sorry for not being there when you and your brother needed me." AJ hugs Aaron a little tighter. "I love you Son and I only want the best for you. I'm trying my best to turn my life around and make things better for your mom and the two of you. Our family is not complete without you and your brother. Will you please come back home so we can figure all this out as a family?" "I'll think about it Pops, I'm not saying NO, but just give me some time," Aaron says. "OK Son, that's fair. Can you at least come out to dinner with us tonight so we can celebrate this big win?" AJ asks him. "Yea I can do that," Aaron says. "Let's go eat. Your mother and brother are probably at the car."

Terrance, now walking towards his car, pulls out his cell phone and makes a call. "Hey what's up Troy? Remember when I told you I ran into AJ Rose? Well, I was at the Crestwood game tonight and his twin boys went off. They should easily win a state title with what I saw tonight! That's not why I'm calling though. I think AJ might be in some serious trouble." "Why you say that?" Troy replies.

"Well, I saw him and his son again tonight and Big Nick had him surrounded with his guys and the conversation didn't look friendly, so I stepped in and tried to calm things down." "Big Nick the d-boy want to be gangster? That Big Nick?" "Yes, the one and the same Troy" "So what happened?" "Well after I stepped in and introduced myself, things kind of cooled off and everyone went their separate ways. I gave AJ a business card and told him if he needed anything to give me a call." "Ok that's a good idea. Who knows what Big Nick is up to..." "Hopefully, AJ will reach out to you," Troy says. "Yea I hope so as well," Terrance exclaims. "I think I should keep my eye on this for a while. I have a feeling, something is off," Terrance adds. "Well, if you feel that strongly about it, by all means do that, and whatever I can do to help, just let me know," Troy says.

After the celebratory dinner, Aaron and AJ walk out the restaurant together as Jamal and Monica hang back, just enough to hear what is being said, but slow enough to give them some space. "That dinner was fire, don't you think son? This is the first time in a long time that we have all been together sitting around a table and just enjoying each other's company like a family. Although I never said this to you all, I have thought about it often." AJ is trying to find the words to convince Aaron how sorry he is about everything and begins to speak from his heart.

"Son you know sometimes as a father, we make mistakes and as a man, we're supposed to own up to our mistakes and take responsibility for our actions. I want to apologize for how I handled this whole situation with Big Nick. I should never have put my hands on you like I did, or raised my fist to you to even gesture that I would hit you. I make no excuses for what I did and I'm truly sorry. I have allowed drugs and alcohol to change me to the point that I lost who I was. I let my upbringing affect your upbringing, you and your brother. Again, I'm not making excuses, I just want you to understand or at least see where I was coming from. It was never my intention to hurt any of you and I will regret that for the rest of my life. I wish I could take back all the negative things you all have endured because of me. Unfortunately, I can't, however what I can do going forward is, be the dad that you can be proud of. I'm working and doing good. I haven't had a drink or did any types of drugs. I'm clean and clear headed for the first time in a very long time. When I did that to you, it terrified me, because I saw my dad in me, and I saw you doing the same thing I did to my dad, and I don't want that to happen. Please forgive me Son. I love you!" The two begin to shed tears as AJ hugs Aaron and squeezes him tight. Aaron is a little reluctant at first, but slowly begins to hug AJ back and whispers, "I love you too Pops!" "Will you come back home Son and we can all start over? "Pops I forgive you, but it's still fresh in my mind. I can't lie, that hurt me Pops… The one man that I have always looked up to was about to smash me! I just need some time, but I will come by and hang out from time to time and maybe eat dinner and we can see where that goes. I kind of like living on my own. Besides, in a few months, I'll be off to college anyway, so I still won't be living there," Aaron says. "Ok, son I understand. If that's what you need, I can respect that. You're definitely becoming a man." Jamal and Monica catch up with AJ and Aaron. "Is everything OK?" she asks. "Yes Mom, everything is OK," Aaron says. "So does that mean you're coming back Bro?" Jamal chimes in. "No, Jamal it just means me and Pops are cool, but we got some things to work out and from time to time, I'll come over and hang out and maybe eat dinner with y'all like a family," Aaron says. "Ok that's what's up." "In the meantime, Bro, we got some work to do if we are going to win state baby! Let's get some shots up in the morning." "Sounds good to me," Jamal agrees. "Let's get this ring!" Jamal states loudly! AJ brings them all in for a family hug.

THE CROSSROADS TO STATE

It's been two weeks since that last game celebration dinner. Everything seems to be getting back to normal, at least for the moment. Aaron and Jamal have been putting in extra work on the court while AJ and Aaron have been trying to put their relationship back together again as well. Everyone is excited for the game this Friday night. As a part of their old routine, Aaron and Jamal decide to get a fresh haircut. As they walk into the salon to Mr. Mon, their barber, they greet all the ladies in the salon and make their way to the basement. "Yo, what it do Mr. Mon," Aaron exclaims… "Aww y'all know me, it's slow motion around this joint." "Yea same here." "Who is going first?" Mr. Mon asks. "I guess I will, since I'm the oldest," says Aaron. "MAN GET OUTTA HERE WITH THAT! You are only older than me by a few minutes!" They all laugh. "Y'all boys ready for that action tomorrow night?" Mr. Mon asks. "Oh, yea," they both say in unison. "Aaron, how's your knee holding up? You gone be good tomorrow night?" "Oh, yea it's all good," Aaron says. "I was scared for a minute there and then I talked with ya Pops, and he was telling me it wasn't as bad as it seemed," Mr. Mon added. "Yea it's all good now. I'm just anxious to get out there.," Aaron reaffirms. "Yea I hear you young buck. Take it from me though, just relax and play your game. Don't try to overdo it. Take it one play at a time and let the game come to you." "Yea I hear you Mr. Mon, you always dropping jewels on us and staying fresh to death with it." "Is that the new J's?" Aaron asked. "Naw man, these old. I just keep them clean. I'm not paying all that money for the same shoe I already got. You have got to remember I'm an old sneaker head. I got all them joints that y'all wearing now." They all laugh. As Mr. Mon finishes Jamal, he tells them both now, "Don't y'all forget what I said about the game and leave my ticket at the gate when y'all make it to the league." He daps them up as they walk back upstairs.

When they get back to the car, Aaron looks at his phone and he's got five missed phone calls from an unknown number. Aaron calls the number back and there's a familiar voice. "Yo, you been ducking me lil dude. You know the line came out today and it's got y'all winning by a dub. You better make damn sure that happens. I need you and your punk ass little brother to win this fucking game or else!! I see you both just got fresh haircuts so you looking fly. You just better not try nothing slick and mess up my money." Aaron looks shaken and tells Jamal to hurry up and get in the car. Jamal could tell something was wrong by the way Aaron's demeanor had changed all of a sudden. Looking all around as of someone was watching. "Aaron what's up bro? Why are you freaking out?" "That was Big Nick; he said the line is out and we have to win by twenty! He also knew we just got our hair cut like he was watching us or something!" Aaron says in a panic, which is making Jamal panic as well. Both of them start looking around to see if anyone is watching. Neither one of them sees anything nor does anyone look suspicious. "Aaron, what are we going to do now?" Jamal asks. "We don't have much of a choice. If we don't do what he says, you know what will happen, not just to us, but to Mom and Pops. We can't go to the police because they work for him too. We right back where we started Bro." "Yea you right. Jamal, I'm sorry I got us into this mess. I just wanted us to have more. We deserved more than to be going hungry. I wanted us to have nice things like everybody else. I guess I got greedy. Having extra money in our pocket, clothes, jewelry, I even got my own car," Aaron says. "Yea, this is nice Bro. Definitely better than catching a ride everywhere we wanted to go; you know when you have your own, it just feels different." "That's one of the reasons why it's so hard to come back home. Having your own spot to come and go and not having anyone to answer is legit. It's like I'm in college a year early and having my own dorm. I have all the perks of being in college without all of the college dorm rules. Not to mention having money in my pocket. Bro I can go eat anywhere I want, buy any pair of shoes I want or outfit I want. Bro I can't lie it feels good not to be broke," Aaron continues. "Aaron I get it. I do, but what happens when that money runs out? Then what will you do?" "I don't know Bro, maybe we will be in college by then and have a NIL deal. Look at how these college athletes are getting paid now. Why can't that be us?" Aaron asks. "It can be Aaron, but we can also do it the right way!" Jamal says. "Well right now, let's just take care of this game and then put all this behind us." "Yea let's get this game over with and get Big Nick out of our lives and move on." "Yea Bro, lets go grab something to eat and watch some film." "Sounds good to me, let's do it," They both agree. "Man, Aaron it's good to be back with you twin. I missed hanging out with you like this," Jamal says. "Yea I know Bro. I missed you Jamall. I promise nothing will ever come between us again," Aaron says. "I'm with that!" Jamal agrees.

It's game day and both Aaron and Jamal are feeling nervous and scared about today. As much as they are focused on the game, both of them seem to be preoccupied. From the moment they walked into school, there was something different in both of them, especially Aaron, who was normally bragging about how good he was going to play, is now quieter and more reserved. At the pep rally, neither had much to say and on the bus ride to the gym, they were even quieter. It wasn't until they walked onto the court that they seemed like themselves. That's when you could see that swagger coming back in Aaron. Jamal just listened to his music, but he was now starting to bob his head and dance a little bit with just subtle moves. Slowly, they began to laugh and talk with the team after they get done warming up. While waiting in the locker room for the game to begin, Aaron's phone begins to vibrate. It's a text message from an unknown number. The text message simply reads, "DON'T FORGET YOU GOT A LOT TO LOSE IF YOU LOSE" Aaron shows the phone to Jamal and then quickly puts it away. Jamal tells Aaron not to worry and just stay focused. "We got this Bro. Stay focused and lock in. It would be hard for anybody to beat the two of us when we are playing together. The team is counting on us, and we have been waiting all our lives to get here and no one is about to take this opportunity from us. Not Big Nick nor anyone else," Jamal says. "I feel you Bro and you're right! Let's get this trophy!" The two of them call the rest of the team together to get everyone going before they take the court. The whole team is hyped up. They huddle up and Aaron screams out, "Family on me….family on three…one, two, three!" They all scream 'family' and take off running towards the court.

The gym is packed with fans and the crowd lets out the loudest cheers as the team takes the floor and starts to go through their warmup routine. AJ and Monica are seated right behind the team's bench with their jerseys on. The team finishes warmups and head back to the bench, awaiting the announcers to call out the starting lineup.

The atmosphere in the gym is electric and everyone is on their feet for the tip off. The referees run to their perspective positions and the head ref heads to center court to start the game. Aaron wins the tip and they run an immediate back pick before Jamal throws the alley-oop for a spectacular windmill thunderous dunk! The crowd goes crazy as Aaron and Jamal celebrate the dunk. However, while those two are celebrating and playing, they don't even notice that Hampton has inbounded the ball and pushed the ball up the court for a layup. The coach instantly calls a timeout and yells for Aaron and Jamal to get to the bench. "Look I don't know what the two of you are on, but whatever it is, you better figure it out now. We celebrate after the game. Get it together and play ball. Am I clear?" the coach exclaims! "Yes Sir," Aaron and Jamal say together. The whistle blows and from that moment on, Aaron and Jamal play lights out. They go on a twenty to two run to end the half with a big three at the buzzer from half court from Jamal; the crowd goes crazy as the team runs off the court and heads back in the locker room. As the team and coaches begin to file in, the coach begins to write on the chalk board, three words, FOCUS, FINISH, FAMILY! Coach begins, "If we plan on being champions, these three words are what I want you to remember. Number one, being focused. Focus on this one half, focus on the next play, focus on what you can control. Number two, Finish. Now let's finish what we started back in the summer. All the training, the running, the weight training, everything you sacrificed to get to this moment. Last but not least is family. This team has truly become a family over the last several months; we have laughed together, cried together and enjoyed a lot of success and now it all comes down to this last half of this game. For some, this is the last game of your high school careers, the last time you will play with each other and the last time I will have the pleasure of coaching you gentlemen. It has indeed been an honor to coach all of you. So, let's go out there and finish what we started. Bring it in…family on me, family on three…one, two, three, FAMILY!" Once again, the team prepares to take the floor. As soon as the team gets back to the bench, Aaron and Jamal look over to AJ and Monica. AJ shouts out, "Let's go boys, you got this." They both smile, nod and taps their heart. AJ returns the tap of the heart.

They start the second half with both teams trading baskets and then Aaron and Jamal both pick up a couple of fouls. They both now have to head to the bench to keep from fouling out of the game. Hampton takes advantage with both of them out and cuts the lead to four at the end of the third quarter. Things have gotten a lot tighter now and the team is becoming unglued, arguing with one another and pointing fingers at one another. What was once a twenty-three point lead for Crestwood is now a six point lead for Hampton. Aaron and Jamal are now panicked as well, because if they don't do what they were told to do, Big Nick will be waiting for them, and their secret will be revealed. "Aaron, Jamal, go check in. Now look, we have to turn the pressure back up, so we will go back to our diamond press, and we are trapping everything especially in the corners, but DO NOT FOUL! On offense, remember we are running motion. Keep the ball moving until we find open shots and don't settle. Aaron and Jamal, look to penetrate and kick if needed. Remember FOCUS, FINISH and FAMILY. Now go and finish this game. On three FINISH!" Coach says as he finishes his pep talk. As the team takes the floor, Hampton takes the ball out and immediately scores, adding to the lead to make it six. Jamal takes the ball out and passes it into Aaron, who walks the ball up the court and calls Jamal over to whispers something in his ear. Jamal takes off, runs down the court and off a few screens before Aaron passes him the ball. Jamal hits a three. Hampton takes the ball out and Aaron gets a steal and a dunk, which ignites the crowd once again. The gym is getting so loud that it becomes deafening. Chants of D-FENSE roars through the crowd almost as if Crestwood were the only school playing. They get another steal and Jamal hits another three. From there, the route was on. Crestwood couldn't miss and Hampton couldn't make a basket. Everything would go in and come right back out. Crestwood safely went up by twenty-five with only seconds on the clock. Jamal takes the ball out, passes it to Aaron one last time and Aaron throws the ball in the air and the clock hits all zeros. They've done it! Everyone rushes the floor. Jamal and Aaron run over to look for AJ and Monica. They all meet on the sidelines and hug. Tears begin to flow from everyone. To finally reach this goal is a dream come true. Flashbacks of all the hard work, the extra sessions, early morning practices, all the extra laps; they have done it. It has all come to fruition and what's better is that they covered the spread without point shaving or doing anything that anyone would suspect. Big Nick would get his money and finally be off their back and now they are free to just enjoy themselves and bask in winning a State Title.

LIFE AFTER BASKETBALL

It's been two months since winning the State Title and Jamal has signed his letter of intent to go to the University of Texas to study law, which was no surprise to anyone. Aaron has decided to stay home and go to the local University. Even though he has had many offers, he felt the need to stay close to home. Although he is still living on his own, his relationship with AJ seems to be better. Monica is now working as a court clerk at the county courthouse and AJ got a promotion. Everything seems to be falling in place for everyone.

One day, Aaron was leaving the gym after getting some shots up; while walking back to his car, some guys approach him and then out of nowhere Big Nick is motioning for Aaron to come over to his car. "Hey, what's up big time? I haven't seen you since the big game. How you been?" Big Nick says. "I been alright," Aaron nervously replies. "Man listen…You and your brother did really good. Congratulations on winning State — that's big! Not to mention we made a lot of money off that game. I hear you did pretty good too!" Aaron asks, "What you mean, what did you hear?" "Boy don't play me like I'm stupid. I got eyes and ears everywhere. I heard you made a come up too. You bet on the game just like I did. Ain't no need to lie to me my boy. In fact, I'm glad you made a little money too. You deserve it! I see you like having a little bread in your pocket too. I think we can make some money together if you are interested," Big Nick says. "Naw man I'm done betting on games. It's too unpredictable, especially with the new team I'll be playing on, they not about that life and with Jamal going away, I can't really count on these guys," Aaron says. Big Nick rebuts, "I'm not talking about that, my boy. I'm talking about you selling weed at the new school. Err body blowing now, and you can be the man they come to. I'll supply you and you can supply the whole campus and the visiting teams when they roll through. I'll have a couple of my people sign up to go to class there to help you out and we can make a killing. If you think that little chump change you won off that game is something, you will have ten times more than that. In fact, I'll give you twenty-five bands right now just to get you going. All you have to do is shake my hand and tell me you're in, that's all and this time what we do stays between me and you. Just think of all the money you will have. You got your scholarship money, the money you made from your bet, not to mention all that money I gave you the first time we did business. I know you still got some of that money left. Bro it's a no brainer. We about to make a killing at the school. By the time you leave school you will be a millionaire and never have to dribble a ball again for the rest of your life unless you want to. Now how does that sound to you?" Big Nick says with excitement. "Man, I don't know," Aaron answers. "What do you mean you don't know? You like making money and having money in your pocket, right? Bro, it's not like I'm asking you to sell crack! This is just weed; everybody is smoking weed these days. Look I'm going to give you fifty thousand right now if you shake my hand and we become partners. I'll front the weed, and you sell it. It will already be bagged and ready to go. Basically, all you're doing is distributing and collecting the money. Simple as that. Do we have a deal? I'm not going to come back to ask again. I don't beg nobody to make money," Big Nick says. Aaron then says, "Ok cool, let's get this money." Aaron shakes hands with Big Nick and takes the duffle bag full of money; the two devise a plan of how they are going to move from here on out.

Later that day is Jamal's going away party. Everybody is going to be there. It's a bittersweet day for the whole family. AJ is just really getting to know the boys and has enjoyed spending time with them. For Aaron and Jamal, this will be the first time in their lives that they will be separated and for Monica, it will be the first time both boys will be out of the house at the same time since she was a teenager. It's a happy occasion, but a sad one at the same time. AJ is in the backyard on the grill cooking for the party when Aaron pulls up with a box for Jamal. Jamal and Monica come out to greet Aaron. "Hey momma, what's good Bro? How are you feeling?" Aaron inquires. "I'm good, a little nervous about going so far away, but excited to get started and get back on the court," Jamal says. "I hear you Bro and you will be just fine. Just remember everything I taught you," Aaron replies. They all laugh. "Here Bro, I have got you a little something to take with you to remind you about home."

"Bro, what is this?" Jamal says excitedly. He rips the paper off and it's a huge 16x20 framed jersey with all his stats from this past season etched in the glass with a picture of the two of them holding that trophy from the state title game. "Bro this is fire… I don't know what to say!" Jamal says with a tear running down his face. "But I didn't get you anything," Jamal then says. "You didn't have to; you are already the best gift I could have ever gotten. You had my back when I needed you the most and you really came through for me. If it weren't for you, I probably wouldn't be here today so this is the least I could do." "Bro this is so dope. I can't wait to hang this in my dorm room. You deserve it Jamal. Yo pops, when is the meat gone be ready so I can get a wing or something off of there while it's still hot?" Aaron says. "Yea come on over Son, I got you. That's a nice gift you got your brother. It looks expensive. It wasn't that bad. I got a good deal on it," Aaron replies. "Yea ok. I'll leave it alone then," AJ says. "How you been Pops?" "I'm good Son. This is probably the best I have felt in a long time. It seems like finally everything is coming together for us. This is definitely the longest period of time I have ever been sober and drug free. So, every day is a blessing and I'm trying to make the most of it," AJ declares. "Hey man, I proud of you! That's what's up! I also been wanting to thank you for standing up for me that night Big Nick and his guys had me cornered," Aaron says. "You don't have to thank me Son. That's what I am supposed to do. I just wish I had been a better father to you boys! If I had, you would never have been in that mess in the first place. I'm just glad it's all over and that things worked out for all of us. If he had hurt either one of you I would have never forgiven myself and would probably be locked up! You haven't had any more problems from him, have you?" AJ asks. "Naw, I haven't even seen him since the game. He got his money and now we are done," Aaron lies. "That's good to hear Son! Big Nick has always been trouble, even when we was kids; he was always getting into something and selling dope. Sooner or later, that lifestyle will catch up with him," AJ says. "Anyway, enough about him, let me get one or two of them wings pops!" Aaron says. AJ checks the wings over and carefully gives Aaron two wings off the grill. "Man, these are fire. Now this is what we need to be selling. We would make a killing!" "Yea I know, but I just don't have the time, the money or the energy to be trying to open up a restaurant or anything like that," AJ says. Just as Aaron was finishing his wings, his teammates began to show up, along with the other kids from school and the neighborhood. Everybody is coming out to say their goodbyes to Jamal. It's a tad bit overwhelming for Jamal with him being such a loner. At the end of the night, Jamal thanks everyone for coming and for their gifts.

After everything is cleaned up, AJ calls everyone into the kitchen. "I just wanted to tell both of you how proud of you I am. Not just for your accomplishments on the court as outstanding as they are; I'm more proud of you for the things you have done off the court and the young men you are becoming. After I blew out my knee, I basically thought my life was over and when your mom had both of you, I was just lost, which is why I took to drinking and doing drugs as a way to escape the pain. I know I was a horrible father, and you have no reason to forgive me or even allow me to be in your life, so I'm grateful for every second that I have with the both of you. It is an honor to be your father. I know I can't go back and fix the past, but from this moment forward, I can do better and be better and I want to start with you Monica." AJ drops to one knee and reaches into his pocket and pulls out a small box. Monica from the first time we met, you have always been my ride or die. You stuck by my side when I was on top, and you stuck by my side when I reached rock bottom. You never gave up on me; even after I gave up on myself, you kept fighting. I can never thank you enough for all that you have done for me and this family. I love you more than I could ever tell you. I know that I don't deserve a second chance; however, I'm going to shoot my shot anyway and ask you. Would you do me the honor of becoming my wife?" Monica can't believe it. Tears are flowing down her face. Both Aaron and Jamal are stunned. A calming quiet has taken over the room waiting for an answer. AJ can hardly contain himself as he awaited the answer. "Yes, Yes, Yes!" Monica screams out as she puts her hand out for AJ to put the ring on her finger. "You know I've waited for a long time to hear those words AJ. I always knew you loved me, and that this day would come." They both hug and kiss. "Well, there is one more thing that I have to ask. Boys, would you do me the honor of being my best men at the wedding?" AJ asks. "Of course, Pops we would love to. Congrats!" "Momma let me see that rock you got there. That's pretty nice Pops." AJ replies, "Yea, I have been waiting for the right time for all of us to be together." "Well, you did that Pops," says Aaron. "Yea you did, I love it!" Monica chimes in. "So, when would you like to get married," AJ asks. "We can get married as soon as possible if you want to. We have waited long enough if you ask me," Monica affirms. "Well, since Jamal is leaving next week, we can do it before he leaves. I don't want a big wedding anyway," AJ says. "So, let's do it!" says Monica. AJ stands up and reaches out to Monica for a hug. He holds her so tight as if to never let go. Tears begin running down his face like an old leaky faucet. Jamal jokingly hands him a roll of paper towels as Aaron Pat's him on the back. "Who would have guessed you're a big softy Pops," Jamal says. They all laugh.

TIME CHANGES ALL

It's been several years since Jamal's going away party. Jamal is finishing up law school, AJ and Monica are now married and seemingly doing well for themselves and Aaron, on the other hand, appears to be doing well- to those who don't travel in his circle. For those who do know him, they know that he is one of the biggest drug dealers in the city. To everyone else, Aaron is a real estate investor. Several years ago, Aaron had made a deal with Big Nick to sell weed for him. They made so much money that it became addicting to him. The more he did it, the easier it got for him. Aaron began to love the lifestyle it afforded him. The money was coming in so fast that he didn't know what to do with it all. He soon had to find a way to clean his money, which led him into real-estate. Aaron became so involved with selling drugs and flipping houses that his basketball career started to take a dive just after his sophomore year. The once-star basketball athlete was now skipping practices, which saw his minutes on the court start to decline. The only thing he did keep up was his grades. He was always so smart that he really didn't have to work that hard at it, which helped him get his degree in accounting and also a real-estate license. On paper, Aaron looked legit. Jamal on the other hand, went the opposite direction. He flourished in Texas both on and off the court. He had become a legitimate pro prospect; however, the pull to help others was greater than his own individual needs. After playing his four years of college basketball, he went into law school without a second thought.

As time went on, his visits home grew less and less. Life begins to happen and phone calls become short; before you know it, space began to creep in and the only way they can keep up with one another is through social media. Life for the Rose's seem to be sweet, even for Monica and AJ, who were living a nice quiet life. Monica started her own business and now works from home; AJ is now coaching little league basketball in his spare time. AJ had always wanted to give back to the youth so what better way for him than to coach little kids, teaching them the game that he loves.

One night after coming home from practice, AJ and Monica are home eating dinner and listening to the news when they hear the late breaking news. *"Former basketball star Aaron Rose has been arrested for money laundering and drug trafficking. We will have more tonight at ten."* "WHAT!?" Monica screams out. "That can't be our Aaron, it can't be. He wouldn't do that!" AJ is looking all around for his cell phone. He's so nervous and frustrated and doesn't see it sitting right in front of him. After a few moments pass, he finally sees it and frantically tries to call Aaron's number. No answer. His phone goes straight to voicemail. He calls again and again. Each time, the call goes unanswered. Monica is freaking out. She doesn't know what to do. AJ fears the worst, but is trying to stay calm in order to help Monica. This is the last thing he thought Aaron would do; sell drugs- after everything their family had been through.

Even though AJ hadn't been in the streets in a long time, he still knew a few people that might know if Aaron had gotten himself into some trouble, so he starts to make a few phone calls. This last call stops him in his tracks. It's confirmed, they did pick up Aaron today for conspiracy to buy and sell drugs. This was AJ's worse nightmare, to see one of his boys behind bars. He instantly drops to his knees. Before he could finish his prayer, his phone rings. It's Aaron. "Hey, what up Pops. Before you ask any questions, yes that was me on the news. I can't talk now, but I'll be by to see you and mom real soon, I promise." "Alright Son, take care of yourself." Monica blurts out, "AJ what in the world is going on? Aaron ain't never sold drugs or anything like that. This has got to be a mistake!" she says. "I know, this makes no sense. All we can do is wait to hear from him. In the meantime. I'm going to give my guy Terrance Mays a call. He's a lawyer, maybe he can help," AJ says. "Good idea," Monica agrees.

"Hello, this is Terrance Brooks," Terrance says as the line rings. AJ is on the line, "Hey, what's up Terrance? This is AJ Rose. I don't know if you saw the news or not, but my son Aaron was arrested today for money laundering and drug charges. I think we may need your services." "Hold on. The one that played basketball and won the State title?" Terrance had to confirm. "Yes that's him. We are not sure what's going on because we haven't been able to talk to him yet. Is this something your law firm could handle?" AJ says. "Yes we can definitely help. I'll tell you what, let me talk to my partners and get back to you probably tomorrow sometime. I know he's out with his family right now," Terrance says. "Ok, thanks Terrance. I really appreciate this." "No problem at all. I'll be talking with you soon, take care," Terrance says before hanging up.

"What did he say?" Monica asks. "He said they could help, but he has to talk with his partners, and he will get back to me sometime tomorrow. Until then we will have to wait until we hear from Aaron," AJ says.

The next morning, Monica and AJ are sitting down and having breakfast when Aaron comes strolling in through the front door. "Good morning Momma, good morning Pops!" Monica runs over to Aaron and hugs him. "What's up Son?" They ask. Aaron begins, "I don't even know where to start. It was my freshman year and Big Nick threatened me again, saying that he would tell the school about what we did. He wanted me to sell weed for him and he gave me fifty thousand dollars. I couldn't turn down that kind of money and I figured since everybody was smoking weed these days, that it wouldn't be a big deal. He set everything up and all I had to do was to let the guys on the team, people around school and even some of the visiting players know where to go when they would come into town. That's all I had to do, was make the introduction and his people would do the rest. I still felt uneasy about doing that, so I went to him and told him I wanted out, and he beat me up pretty bad. That's the real reason why I missed some practices and my love for basketball started to fade away. After that, he had heard that I was good with numbers, and he told me that if I helped him move his money around and clean it, then we could call it even. So, I showed him how if he bought some abandoned homes that he could use his dirty money to fix them up, inflate the cost of material for fixing the houses and then sell the houses; he could clean his money that way. The only problem with that was he couldn't put his name on the properties, and I couldn't put them in my name, so Nick brought in this guy named Anthony Roberts. You may have heard of him; he is a lobbyist and does a lot of stuff around town. Anthony and I would find different properties to buy. I would crunch the numbers and then Anthony and Big Nick would make the purchases. I never got involved in that part of their business and from time to time, I would find some properties for myself and put the house in one of the guys from school's name and give him a few grand and keep it moving. I had a knack for it, which is how I ended up selling real-estate. Now from what I have gathered so far from all of this, is that there is some federal investigation going on with sex trafficking young women, murder, extortion, drugs, money laundering and a lot of other stuff that I'm not even aware of with some pretty high-level individuals like senators, presidents of banks, school officials and God knows who else. I'm just a small fish in this ocean of illegal activities," Aaron drops the bombshell. "Oh my GOD what the hell have you gotten yourself into?" AJ responds. "I don't know Pop. I haven't done anything for some time now and all of a sudden, this stuff is coming out of nowhere. I still don't know how they connected me in any of this. My name isn't on anything. Even with the properties that I had bought and sold back, they went under someone else's name. I never did any hand-to-hand buys or take any money from anyone." "Well Son, do you have a lawyer?" Aaron says replies, "I called Jamal to see if he could help, but he didn't pick up. I was also thinking about calling your guy Terrance. I can't think of his last name, but I remember him, and his partner got that lady off that was involved in that murder case." "Well, when your mom and I had heard the news, we called him. He told me that he would talk to his partner Troy and get back to me. We are waiting on him to call us back sometime later today," AJ says. "Aaron why would you keep dealing with that dude? You know he ain't nothing but trouble," AJ goes on to ask. "I know Pops, but I couldn't pass up fifty grand just for making an introduction. I wanted to do things on my own so bad that I just got caught up in that fast money," Aaron says. His father adds, "I know all too well how easy it is to get caught up in that life." Just then, Jamal calls Monica's phone. "Hey what's going on? I got Aaron's message saying he had be arrested? What's going on?" Monica replies and says, "Well, I will let Aaron explain it all to you." "Aaron it's Jamal on the phone." Jamal acknowledges, "Hey what's up Bro?" Aaron begins to tell Jamal everything that has happened. "Aaron, what were you thinking messing with that dude again after all he had done to us and our family? Come on man!" Jamal exclaims over the phone. "I know Jamal and that's why I stopped working with him. All this is coming out of nowhere. I don't know what to do and I could use your help," Aaron says. "I'm sorry that you're going through this Bro, and I already booked a flight home. I'll be there in the morning. In the meantime, don't talk to anyone and don't do anything until I get there, and we can come up with a plan," Jamal says. "I know Jamal. Oh, Mom and Pops already talked with an attorney, he is supposed to be calling us later today," Aaron adds. "Who did they talk to?" Jamal asks. "They talked to Terrance Mays, he is a friend of Pops. He and his partner are supposed to be two of the best lawyers in the city." "Ok well maybe we all can sit down and talk to figure this thing out," Aaron says. "Sounds good bro. I can't wait to see you. It's been too long. Tell Mom and Pops I love them, and I'll see you all tomorrow," Jamal says before hanging up.

Aaron relays the message, "Jamal says he will be here tomorrow, and we can all sit down and talk to figure things out.

Man, Pops, why does it feel like every time life seems to be going good for me, things are working out just like we planned then life throws you a curveball and everything seems to fall apart? I've tried to be a good person, I help other people, I give to the needy, I'm a good person Pops, I really am!" Aaron says with a shaky voice. AJ moves in to hug and console Aaron. He buries his face in his father's chest and begins to weep uncontrollably. "It's ok Son, we will get through this," AJ reassures Aaron. You know Son, things happen for a reason and we can't always see that reason or understand why. I do know that there is a lesson in all of this and a purpose for it all. We just have to trust God and know that His plan is working for our good. Maybe one day you will have to share your testimony, and that testimony will help someone to not go through what you're going through right now. I know it feels like the world is against you right now Son and I know this is hard. Believe me I do, you will get through this and when you get on the other side, you're going to be a better man. One thing though Son. You can't live one life in the streets and the other one trying to do what's right. You have to be all in one way or the other. No person can serve two masters, as they say," AJ says to him. "I know pop and I promise I'll do better," says Aaron. "I know you will Son and we will get through this together." The next morning Aaron and AJ are sitting around the table eating breakfast and Aaron feels the need to get some things off his chest. You know Pops, after our talk last night I did some soul searching and you were right. I was trying to live a double life and serve two masters. I thought I could do the street thing and do what's right as long as I didn't hurt nobody. All I could see was the dollar signs and not being broke. Money has ruled my thoughts for as long as I can remember, and the more I got, the more I wanted. I was addicted to it. I needed it, I wanted it, and I couldn't get enough of it. It ruled every thought and decision that I made. I can see that now and how wrong I was in my thinking. WOW

Aaron, that is probably the realest statement I have ever heard you make. It takes a real man to hold himself accountable like you just did. I'm so proud of you son. AJ says with tears in his eyes.

Three months has passed, and Jamal has now joined Brooks and Mays law firm in assisting with Aaron's case. After some discovery and their own investigation, they have learned that Aaron was being set up from the start. Everything Aaron thought he knew was far from the truth. There were no documents with Anthony Richardson's name on it anywhere. Every document that was turned over to them in discovery only had Aaron's name on it, from banking papers, title loan papers, even a fake LLC that was created with Aaron's name on it. Terrance is perplexed by all of this. It all sounds familiar, but he's not sure why. "Maybe we should ask Mr. Roberts some questions at his office," Jamal says after going over the papers and coming up with nothing. "No not yet. You have to pass the bar here in Illinois first. You keep working on that and we will let our private detective do some digging into Mr. Roberts. We need to find out who he is connected to before we do anything. We don't want to be blindsided by anything or anyone. This is bigger than just Aaron and it's got some heavy hitters behind it," Terrance explains. "Let's take a step back and look at all the people involved in this. Maybe we are looking at things too closely. We have Big Nick, his two goons who control the money and the drugs; the title company owner, the bank president / mortgage broker and Anthony Roberts the lobbyist. He's probably the one who connects everyone together. Hey, wait a minute, look at this. I just googled the president of the bank, his name is Walter Jones, and his wife Patricia Jones is the owner of the title company. Walter gets approvals for all the real-estate loans. Although his name doesn't appear on any paperwork, he has to be the one that brokers the loans. His wife then does the paperwork for the houses and there you have it. Big Nick is in business. This is probably how they got all of Aaron's information and signature. When he was buying his own personal property he signed his paperwork, and they just photocopied his papers, so it looks like he signed it all." "That's great work Jamal," Terrance says. "If we can prove this, that would take care of the money laundering case, right? What about the drug case?" Aaron nervously questions. "This is just off the top of my head, but I think we can possibly get you off on that or at least probation. Now don't hold me to this… All I'm saying is that we have a shot," Terrance says. "At this point, I'll take it Terrance, thank you," Aaron replies.

Just as Terrance was wrapping up their meeting, he gets a phone call from Troy. "Hey what's up Terrance, sorry I couldn't make the meeting today," Troy says. "It's ok, I understand you wanting to go to Tre's doctor appointment with Jasmine. How did it go?" Terrance asks. "Everything was good. The doctor says that Tre is completely healed, and he doesn't see any long-term effects." "That's good to hear. I'm glad nephew is doing well," says Terrance. Troy then asks, "How did the meeting go with Aaron and Jamal?" "It went well. Jamal is going to be a fine lawyer once he passes the bar. Maybe we can take him on as an associate. Anyway, after some digging, we discovered that Aaron had been set up on the money laundering charges. The guy that Aaron was working with, his name is Anthony Roberts; he is the connection between Big Nick and the properties. Walter Jones is the broker for the mortgage loans and his wife Patricia Jones, is the title lender. She had all of Aaron's information and was putting his name on everything," Terrance says. *"Wait a minute,"* Jasmine says in the background. *"Did you say Anthony Roberts? That's the lobbyist right? I think I know that name. I'm working on something now. Do you remember the lady that came into the office after the Senator Johnson murder trial?"* "Yea I do," Terrance says. "I think all of us may need to sit down and go over both of these cases. This Anthony Roberts character might be at the center of both cases or at the very least, he knows something about both cases with him being a lobbyist and your case is dealing with the Senators and sex trafficking. It makes sense," says Terrance. "Jasmine, you and Troy should get back to Tre. I'll talk to you both later. Give nephew a big hug for me," Terrance adds.

They all say their goodbyes. Aaron and Jamal walk out together before Aaron turns to Jamal. "Bro, do you think I have a chance, knowing what we know now?" "Yes, I definitely think you have a chance to beat this. We just have to connect the dots and get proof of everything we are alleging. It's going to be a process and unfortunately, the wheels of justice often turn very slow. Trust and believe though that we will get through this. For now you have to keep your head down and stay out of trouble. Outside of us, don't talk to anybody about this case or what we have just learned," Jamal says.

"Bro there is one thing that I have been meaning to talk to you about or say to you for some time now. I wanted to apologize for my actions and behavior over the years.

I realize that I was the main cause of our family splitting up the way we did and that I not only put all of you in danger; I put my own hopes and dreams above yours and forced you into a situation that was detrimental to you. I was reckless with my behavior and my mouth. I sincerely apologize from the bottom of my heart," Aaron says, as tears begin to flow as he continues to apologize. Jamal begins tearing up as well and says, "It's OK Bro, I understand why you did what you did back then. You did what you thought was best considering how we were living." "Man, Bro I have been wanting to tell you this for so long," Aaron repeats. "Aaron, I know you would never do anything to hurt me intentionally or Mom and Pops." Just as Aaron and Jamal began to embrace one another, Aaron falls to the ground and blood begins to fill the back of his white shirt Aaron has been shot in the back and appears to have come out on his side but there is so much blood that he can't tell how bad it is! Jamal quickly falls to his knees as he rolls Aaron over. The front of his shirt is now soaked with blood. Jamal screams out, "Help me! Help me! Somebody help me!!!" Terrance hears Jamal's cry for help and immediately runs out to help while calling 9-1-1. A few minutes later, the ambulance arrives and rushes him to the hospital. AJ, Monica, Jamal and Terrance are anxiously awaiting to hear something from the doctors. Hours have now passed and still no word. The stress of it all has AJ on edge. He wants to go get high to help ease his anxiety; yet he knows what it would do to not only him, but his whole family. The grip of his addiction grows tighter and tighter. He blames himself for everything that is going wrong. Monica can feel that something is going on with AJ. She tries to calm him, but nothing is working. She automatically goes into prayer. "Heavenly Father, I thank you that you always hear me. I come to you now as humble as I can. First, thank you for all that you have done thus far. I thank you that you have kept us. Right now, I come to you on behalf of my husband. Father, touch him right now where he stands in the need of. I know right now, it's a difficult time for him and a lot to deal with, so Father I pray that you give him a sense of peace. Father, I pray that you remove the taste for drugs and alcohol. Father, I pray that he learns to give himself some grace. Father, remind him that we all fall short and that all we have to do is ask and it shall be given. Father, then I ask that you touch Aaron. Give strength where he is weak. Lord, you know every inch of his body better than any doctor ever could. Right now I come asking on behalf of myself and his father that you be in the operating room. Touch every doctor, every nurse, everyone that has anything to do with his care. Lastly Lord, I pray that you even touch the one who pulled the trigger and shot my baby. Touch his heart and his mind so that he will do the right thing and turn himself in to the authorities. Father, I pray that you touch each and every one of us. Allow us to be the good stewards that you have called us to be. In your Son's Jesus name I pray, amen."

"Amen and thank you my love," AJ replies. "I needed that more than you could ever know. I could feel the enemy pulling me back to my old ways and to be honest, I was thinking about it. Then you began to pray and somehow I found the strength to pull away and now I have this sense of peace. Aaron is going to be just fine. We just have to hold…" Before AJ could finish his thought, the doctor comes through the doors. "Mr. & Mrs. Rose, I'm Dr. Craig and I was just in surgery with Aaron and it's still fifty/fifty. The bullet did a lot of damage. If Aaron does come out, he may not walk again. He may be paralyzed from the waist-down." AJ turns to the doctor and says, "Doc, with all due respect to you and what you have learned in school, I don't accept that. My GOD is a healer and a way maker. You do what you have to and what you have learned in school and I'm going to do what I need to do according to my faith. My faith tells me that my Son will be OK and he will walk and live a normal life, just like he did before he was shot. If he delivered me from my addictions and demons, then HE CAN AND WILL DO THE SAME FOR MY SON!" The doctor turns to him and says, "Amen I'm in total agreement with you Mr. Rose. I'm glad you and your family believe. I stand with you in faith!"

Later that night, Aaron begins to stir, and Jamal is right there by his side. "Take it easy Bro, don't try to move too much." Aaron says, "What's going on? What am I doing here? What happened?"

Jamal finally tells him, "Bro, you were shot in a drive-by. We didn't see who it was, but it had to be some of Big Nick's people. Hold on Bro, let me go get the doctor and let them know you're awake." While Jamal is getting the doctor, AJ and Monica walk into the room. "Son, you're awake!" AJ exclaims! "How are you feeling?" "I'm in some pain, but to be honest, it's not that bad, must be the medication that they got me on," Aaron says. Dr. Craig then walks in on the conversation. "Aaron, you're a lucky man, how you doing?" Aaron replies, "I'm in some pain, but other than that, I'm good, I think." "Ok, well that's good," The doctor says. Then Aaron turns to his brother, "Jamal, can you put some socks on my feet? They feel a little cold." Dr. Craig intervenes. "Aaron, are you sure your feet are cold? Yea Doc, they feel a little weird and they are cold." the doctor then says, "Ok…. Aaron, can you move your toes for me?" "I'm trying to Doc, but I can't. What's going on Doc? WHY CANT I FEEL MY LEGS OR MY FEET?" Aaron begins to panic. Doc responds, "Aaron, the bullet did a lot of nerve damage, and we did the best we could to repair most of it; however, we couldn't repair all of the damage." Aaron's face is now flush, "Doc what are you telling me right now!? Are you saying that I am paralyzed?" "Unfortunately, Aaron, we don't know as of yet. It's going to take some time for you to heal and then we will go from there." "Doc this can't happen! I have too much going on. What can I do? I can't be paralyzed!" Aaron begins to hit his legs and starts crying. Tears begin streaming down his face as he hits his legs harder and harder. Dr. Craig and AJ rush in to stop him. "Aaron, you have to calm down, please you're only going to make things worse by doing this. You have to calm down." AJ moves in and hugs Aaron in order to comfort him. Aaron grips AJ and continues to cry uncontrollably, squeezing AJ tighter and tighter. "We will get through this Son, I promise we will. GOD can perform miracles Son and He will see you through this." Monica and Jamal move closer to the bed. They all hug Aaron and let him know that they all are here for him and that they will work together to get through this as a family.

Six months have passed, and Aaron is trying to wrap his mind around being paralyzed, and the possibilities of being in a wheelchair for the rest of his life. Not to mention, he is still facing jail time. As hard as he is trying to stay positive and find the good in all of this, he finds himself slipping into a deep depression and it's starting to show in his appearance and in his demeanor. He tries to blame it on being in the wheelchair, but he is not eating very much, and his drinking has increased dramatically. He's up to a liter of vodka a day, putting it in his coffee or orange juice in the morning during the day and mixing it in cranberry juice in the evening, sometimes even drinking it straight. Aaron is on the edge of losing his purpose and falling into that dark place where nothing and no one matters, including himself. Jamal sees how Aaron is slowly giving up, but he doesn't want to accept it. He feels powerless to stop it, but he knows he has to do something before he loses Aaron forever. He decides to confront Aaron about his drinking and tries to remind him that he has every reason in the world to fight and not to give up.

"Aaron we need to talk. I have noticed that lately you have been different. You haven't said one word about your case, and you don't even ask about how the case is going. You sit around and drink all day to the point you pass out in that chair," Jamal says. "What are you talking about Jamal? Ain't nobody drinking," Aaron says. "Aaron, come on Bro, are you seriously going to sit here and lie to me of all people? I know you better than anyone. I can see how you have changed. Mon hasn't cut your hair in months; you haven't bathed in at least a couple of days, and I can smell the alcohol from way over here," Jamal says. "Jamal, ain't nobody drinking like that. I may have had a couple of drinks, but it wasn't that much. As far as getting my haircut, I haven't had a ride to the barbershop to see Mon. You know it's not easy being stuck in this wheelchair. Trying to maneuver in and out the bathroom is not easy either." "If that's the case Aaron, then why haven't you asked for help? Why is your water bottle filled with vodka? Come on Bro, I know you! LET ME HELP YOU!" Jamal insists. Aaron replies, "Jamal, I don't need any help, what don't you understand? I'm good, I don't know what else I can tell you." "Ok If that's true, then you won't mind if we get you cleaned up and pour out all this vodka you got stashed around the house," Jamal says sarcastically. "Go right ahead, I'm not tripping," Aaron snaps back!

Meanwhile back in the office Troy and Terrance are having a conversation. "Troy, have you noticed how the phone has been ringing off the hook? It's been crazy ever since Senator Johnson's murder trial." Troy answers "Yes I've noticed and if we keep growing like this, we will have to get more attorneys to join the firm. Our case load is already out of hand. I think I see Jasmine more in court than I do at home," says Troy. "Excuse me Mr. Brooks, Mr. Mays, there is a Special Agent Goodloe on the phone. He said that he would like to speak to you both if possible," The secretary says. "That's fine, put him through." "Hello, this is Troy Brooks and Terrance Mays, what can we do for you?" The Agent says, "Well I would rather not get into any specifics over the phone. Would it be possible if we could meet in person? We can meet here at our field office or I can come to your office. Whichever is easier for the two of you?" "Ok, well I have court until 3:30 what about you Terrance?" Troy says. "I should be done around then as well," says Terrance. "Well Special Agent Goodloe, how about we meet at 4pm here at our office. I'll send you our address." The agent responds, "No need, I already have it." "Ok we will see you at four," says Troy. Terrance hangs up the receiver. "What is that about I wonder?" "I don't know Terrance, but I am curious as to what he wants." "So am I, especially since we don't have any Federal cases at the moment. Well we can't sit here racking our brains Troy, let's go handle the cases we do have and figure this out later," Terrance replies.

It's three forty-five now and both Troy and Terrance are back in the office; Troy calls Jasmine into the office and explains everything to her. Just as Troy finishes telling Jasmine what's going on, the secretary knocks on the door. "Special Agent Goodloe is here to see you," she tells the three of them. "Ok great, can you take him into the conference room please?" Troy directs her.

"Hello Agent Goodloe. I'm Troy Brooks, these are my partners. Terrance Mays and Jasmine Jones." "Well I won't beat around the bush. I'm the lead investigator in a federal case that I believe you guys, or should I say your client, Aaron Rose, has stumbled his way into," Agent Goodloe says. "What do you mean?" Troy asks. "Well let me start from the beginning. Remember the murder case you had involving Senator Johnson? Well we had been investigating him for some time. The Senator and some other very powerful people, are… or should I say, were involved in a sex and female trafficking ring. The Senator was heavily involved." "Ok, but what does that have to do with us?" Terrance asks. "Well this man…" Special Agent Goodloe pulls out his phone and shows him a picture of Aaron, "…who I believe is your client, correct?" "Yes he is our client," Terrance exclaims. "Well, we had been surveying this guy…" he shows him a picture of Big Nick "…And Aaron's name came up on a wire tap. We don't think that Aaron has anything to do with our investigation, but because of his relationship with

Big Nick, we were hoping he would help us get these guys and put them away for a long time," the agent says. "Well why come to us?" Troy asks. "Well we are aware of Aaron's legal troubles and we would be willing to help him with those if he would be willing to help us with our investigation. I'll leave you my information and let you talk it over with your client and then you all can give me a call and we can go from there. Also, please remind your client that this case is under investigation so please do not breathe a word about this to no one." "Yes, we will make it clear that he is not to talk to anyone about this investigation," Terrance replies. "Great, I look forward to working with you all," says Special Agent Goodloe. "Wow, can you believe that? I think we are caught right in the middle of this," Jasmine says. "What do you mean?" Terrance replies. "This all starts with Senator Johnson's death and everything we found out about what he was doing. Remember we read the diary of Ms. Boudreaux's daughter who committed suicide. What if it wasn't suicide and she was actually murdered, and the Senator and his friends covered it up? Not to mention… remember when Ms. Melody aka Mel came into the office right after the trial and wanted our help? Remember how scared she was and how she had been hiding out, running from the Senator and his friend?" "Oh yea I see where you're going Jasmine," Troy chimes in. "This could get very dangerous for Aaron. We will have to be extremely careful in how we move from this point," Troy reminds them. "Agreed but I'm not sure if Aaron will go for it," says Terrance. "You know the rule about snitching." What rule? Jasmine ask, "Snitches get stitches," Troy and Terrance say at the same time. "OMG, this could help Melody too. She could outline the whole operation and give the Feds everything they need while helping us get Aaron off," Jasmine says. "Do you think Aaron would go for it Terrance?" Troy asks. "He will if he wants to get off of these charges," Terrance replies. "I'll call him in the morning and set up a meeting to go over all of this. We should reach out to Jamal as well since they are identical twins. "

The following morning, Aaron rolls off of the couch, still in last night's clothing. He had been up all-night drinking and when he looks at his phone, he sees that he has missed ten phone calls from Jamal and five from Terrance. Aaron struggles to pull himself up to the couch and then he calls Jamal back. "Hey, what's up Bro. Sorry I missed your call. I couldn't find my phone, somehow it fell underneath the couch. Anyway, what's up?" "Terrance and Troy may have a way out for you. They need you to come to the office so that they can tell you all about it. Get dressed now and I'll be on my way to pick you up in a few minutes. Ok I'll go get ready and be waiting on you," Aaron replies.

Terrance and Troy are in the conference room waiting for Special Agent Goodloe to be led in. "Good morning gentlemen. Have you talked to your client yet?" "No not yet," Terrance replies. "We wanted to talk to you first and find out exactly what you want Aaron to do and what kind of guarantees do we have that you will help us." "Well I figured you both would say that, so I took up the liberty to draw up these papers stating that if Aaron helps us with the investigation, then all charges will be dropped, and no further actions will be taken towards him. As I stated before we never really wanted him. We want Big Nick. If we get him, we can flip him and bring down the rest. So far, he has been untouchable, and no one has been able to infiltrate his organization. Since Aaron was already a part of his crew, he could get back in and help us get more information on the other major players. Now if you look on the last page at the bottom, you will see I've already signed it. Your client just has to agree, and he can be a free man by this afternoon." "That's easy for you to say Agent Goodloe," Troy says. Just then,

Jamal knocks on the conference room door. "Hey, can I speak to you guys really quick?" he asks. "Sure," Terrance replies. "We will be right back Special Agent," says Troy. "Hey what's up? Did you get Aaron?" "Yes, I picked him up." "What is it?" Troy remarks. "Well he looks terrible and smells even worse. Apparently, he had been up all-night drinking. Your secretaries are giving him some coffee right now to help sober him up. Let me apologize for him and his actions before we even get started. Ever since he was shot, he has been spiraling on this downward path. He was already difficult and now he is impossible to deal with at times," Jamal warns. "No need to apologize Jamal, we get it and have dealt with people like Aaron before," Troy tries to set Jamal at ease. "You guys ready to go do this?" Terrance asks. "Good morning Aaron, it's good to see you again," Terrance says. "It's good to be seen. I thought I was a goner for a second there," Aaron says. "I hear you man. You remember my partner Troy right?" "Yea I remember him, how you doing?" "I'm good Aaron, thank you." Jamal tells me that you may have some good news for me? Aaron says. "Yea we do possibly have a way to keep you out of going to court and out of jail." "That's what's up! Man, I had a good feeling about y'all." "Not so fast Aaron, there is something you need to know." "Aww shit! I should have known there is always a catch. What, I got to do wear a wire or some shit like that? I ain't no damn snitch. Do y'all know what happens to snitches in my neighborhood? They get stitches or wind-up dead. If that's why y'all called me down here, you can forget it. Jamal you ain't been gone that long, you know how Big Nick get down… Man get me the fuck out a here. I'll take my chances at trial and going to jail," Aaron strongly expresses himself. "Aaron, calm down and let me explain it all to you before you make up your mind." "Naw fuck that Troy! I'm not a SNITCH!!!! WHAT DON'T YALL UNDERSTAND!!! JAMAL YOU ALREADY KNOW WHAT IT IS BRO! HOW YOU BE

DOWN WITH ME BEING A SNITCH? YOU OF ALL PEOPLE! YOU COULD HAVE TOLD ME THIS SHIT AT THE HOUSE AND SAVED EVERYBODY A TRIP," Aaron exploded. "Aaron, please if you just give me a second to go over your deal and explain how we can pull this off and get all of your charges dropped. Oh, yea we have it in writing as well right now. You see this paper here. This is your deal signed and sealed, dropping all the cases against you today if you agree to help them bring down Big Nick. They don't want you and they want him. He is a part of something much bigger than we even knew. The FBI will be watching over you and could possibly put you in a witness protection program. We haven't asked them yet, but we could. Look, there are a lot of lives at stake here, not just yours. They are into drugs, sex, and female trafficking from what I understand. You would be helping a lot of people, Aaron. Now what they don't know is that we have another witness who has first-hand knowledge of all the trafficking crimes along with names and numbers of some pretty powerful people. What if we can trade your testimony for her testimony and still get you the deal? Would you be ok with that?" Troy asks. "If you can do that, then hell yea we can do that. As long as I don't have to be a snitch I'm down," Aaron says. "Ok, so listen, this is how we are going to play this. Special Agent Goodloe is going to come into this room. We will introduce the two of you and then we will begin to negotiate the terms and then you can tell him that you will cooperate with the investigation. From there we will tell Special Agent Goodloe that we found another witness who is willing to testify about the entire operation. Once he sees how much information we have, he will have to sign off on the deal; therefore, getting all your charges dropped." Aaron seems relieved and says, "OK I'm with that, as long as I don't have to snitch or wear a wire, none of that," Aaron demands. "Ok, well I'll go get Agent Goodloe and we can get these charges dropped for you. I'll be right back," Terrance explains.

"Agent Goodloe, this is our client Aaron Rose." "Good morning Mr. Rose, nice to meet you. I hear we have an agreement, is that right?" Agent Goodloe says with a smile. Terrance immediately jumps in… "Yes, we do have an agreement. However, there is a little bit of a change. Our client won't be the one testifying," Terrance says. "Wait a minute, hold up! You said we had a deal! I'm confused. What's going on? You all trying to play me?" Agent Goodloe is now getting annoyed. "No not at all," Terrance chimes in. "Since the last time we met with you, we have found some new information that we think will be more beneficial to you than what Aaron has to say," Terrance explains. "Now agent Goodloe, you stated that it's not our client that you want, correct?" "Correct," he admits. "You also said you wanted information that can help you bring down the whole organization. Right? Well we now have a witness who can give you information on the whole operation. They have names, dates, phone numbers, everything. Our witness not only worked for Senator Johnson, she also worked with the Senator trafficking young women and drugs. She is willing to testify if you give her immunity and place her and her child in the witness protection program. She wants a fresh start. You not only get Big Nick; you get some other very powerful people. Everything you wanted from Aaron, just through another person. How does that sound?" "Sounds like it might be something we can swing. I'll have to call my boss and get his approval," Agent Goodloe says. "That's fine," Troy remarks. "We would also have to verify their story," Agent Goodloe adds. "No problem, we can do that and bring the witness and evidence to you this afternoon. Do we have a deal?" Troy says with confidence. "Yes I believe we do," Agent Goodloe responds. "Aaron, you good with all this?" "Oh most definitely!" Aaron says with an excited tone. "Ok great. Aaron, sign here, here and here and we are all set. Aaron you're a free man," Troy says. Aaron breaks down and begins to shed tears of joy. Jamal thanks agent Goodloe for giving Aaron another chance and then thanks Terrence and Troy for working with them and believing in them.

"Now all we have to do is get Melody on board," Troy says.

Troy pulls out his cell phone to call Melody. The phone rings and rings with no answer. Troy tries again and again and gets the same results. He calls Jasmine next in hopes that they are either together or she has talked with her. "Hey Troy, I was just about to call you. I was just about to leave from Mel's," Jasmine says. "Oh ok good." "Why what's up? What happened with Special Agent Goodloe?" Troy responds, "He said he had to check with his superiors, but it's just a formality. Is Mel willing to testify still?" Troy asked anxiously. "Yes, she wants this over with." "GREAT, that's great news. Everyone gets what they want. We help Mel and Aaron…." Just as Troy is expressing his happiness, a loud explosion goes off in the background. "Jasmine! …. Jasmine hello? …. Hello? Baby talk to me!!!! Jasmine!!!" Troy is yelling in the phone with no answer. Terrance rushes over to Troy. "What's going on Troy? What happened… talk to me man!" "I don't know. One minute I was talking to Jasmine and then I heard an explosion and now nothing; I'm only getting a busy signal. We got to go!!! I HAVE TO GET TO HER T!!!" "Do you know where she is?" "No, I don't, she didn't want anyone to know Mel's location," Troy replies with a trembling voice. "Ok well you got that app on your phone to track her location right?" "Yea I think I do. I've never used it before though," Troy replies. "Here, let me see it. I got you bro."

Terrance and Troy speed over to Jasmine's location according to the app on the phone. When they pull up, fire crews are on the scene and a roaring fire that firefighters are fighting with. Through the smoke, Troy sees what looks like it could be Jasmine's car turned upside down. "NOOOOOOOO NOOOOO!!!!!" Troy screams and jumps out the car and runs towards what appears to be Jasmine's car. The firefighters stop him just as he approaches the car. He doesn't see anyone. Troy begins to panic, yelling her name. "Jasmine, Jasmine!!! Then out of nowhere through the smoke, a shadow runs toward Troy with open arms. It's Jasmine! Troy is so relieved! "Oh MY GOD LOVE! I thought I had lost you! What happened?" Jasmine responds, "I don't know, I was sitting in the car talking to you and the next thing I remember is being pulled out my car upside down." "Oh my GOD, Troy where is Mel? She was in the house," Jasmine says terrified as she is thinking the worst. Terrance rushes off to talk to the EMTs and firefighters. "Has anyone seen another young lady? African American about five foot five, approximately one-hundred thirty pounds?" Terrance inquires. "No sir. We haven't found anyone as of yet to my knowledge." Just then, a call comes over the radio.' *We have one victim who appears to be a Black female in her twenties found unconscious with second and third degree burns all over. Captain we got another victim here as well. Victim appears to be a small child nonresponsive.'* Terrance drops his head and heads back towards Troy and Jasmine. "Well I think they've found Mel and her baby. Mel has been badly burned and her child didn't make it," Terrance explains to Jasmine and Troy. Jasmine's body goes limp and she falls toward the ground; Troy and Terrance call for help. The EMTs come rushing over and begin to check Jasmine's vitals. They're concerned that she may have a concussion and they need to rush her to the hospital. "T, can you stay here and try to figure out what happened here? I'm going to go to the hospital with Jasmine." "Yes sure Troy, I got you bro. You go handle your business with Jasmine Bro. I'll handle things here."

Terrance takes out his cell phone and calls Agent Goodloe. "Hello, we might have a problem. There was an explosion at the house we were keeping our witness at; now she is critically burned with second and third degree burns. She is in critical condition. The EMTs said that she had a fifty/fifty chance of recovering. She is being rushed to the hospital on State St. as we speak. I'll call you later if we hear anything else," Terrance says. "I'm sure you know this already, but if she can't help us get Big Nick, then our deal is off and we go right back to our original deal with your client becoming a snitch. Are we clear Mr. Mays?" "Yes… we are crystal clear, Agent Goodloe!" Terrance says.

Later that night. Troy and Terrance are sitting in Jasmine's hospital room where she is being kept for observation. Terrance phone rings. "Special Agent Goodloe, what can I do for you?" "I'm calling to see if there are any changes in your witness' condition?" "Yes, she is doing much better," Terrance replies. "Well I'd like to come see her tomorrow and get the information that you promised me. By the way, what is her name and what room number is she in?" Agent Goodloe asks. "Her name is Melissa Johnson and she is on the third floor, room A four." "Ok great, I will see you all tomorrow at ten a.m." "Yes, see you tomorrow."

"Was that him, T?" Troy asks. "Yes, that was him. He asked me what's her name and your hunch was right… He is not working for the FBI. Is everything in place?" Troy responds – "Yes all of the civilians are off the floor and replaced with real agents," Terrance says. "Good," Troy replies. It's now three a.m. and it's extremely quiet, when a single orderly gets off the elevator with a mop and a bucket. His face is covered with a mask. His shoes are covered by booties, with rubber gloves on his hands. He slowly makes his way to room A four. He checks all around to see if anyone is watching then sneaks into the room and sees a body all wrapped up in bandages from head to toe with an IV in one of the arms. He eases his way over and pulls out a syringe, injecting the IV with a clear liquid. When he turns around to walk out of the room, there are dozens of FBI agents now on the floor with guns drawn. "Special Agent Goodloe, you are under arrest for attempted murder. Thank you, Mr. Mays & Mr. Brooks, we will honor your deal for Aaron and thank you for the diary. We will put that information to good use," says the arresting officer. "You're more than welcome."

"So Troy, how and when did you figure this all out? How did you know he was dirty?" Terrance asks. "Well the first thing was, he signed the fake offer before he even gave it to us. That's like writing a blank check and endorsing it. The next thing was he never asked for any kind of proof of what information we could possibly give him. That all made me a little uneasy. So I called a friend of mine in the FBI and asked him about the investigation and Special Agent Goodloe and it turns out that he is not on that investigation team. That's when we came up with our plan to switch it up on him. Oh and remember when he asked you about what room she was in and what is her name? Like you said, we never told him that our witness was a male or female. When you told me that, I knew we had him and it was just a matter of time before he slipped up," Troy says. "Wow, Troy he really had me fooled," Terrance says. "It happens Bro. We wanted to help Aaron so badly that we both were fooled," Troy says. "What about Melody?" "Oh, she is fine and her child is too. Both of them were dummies and the academy award goes to Jasmine Jones for her role in this action thriller. Sorry we couldn't tell you earlier about our little rouse, but we didn't know if the office or our homes were bugged… which my friend will be doing a sweep of in the morning, so don't be talking dirty on the phone tonight." "Oh you got jokes Huh?" "That's you and Jasmine texting on the phone," Terrance says. They all begin laughing. "Well… good night y'all."

Back at home with their parents Aaron calls them all into the living room. First, I want to say thank you to all of you for having my back throughout the years. Even when I didn't deserve it you all were still there for me. Pops all my life I wanted to be just like you. Now I can understand why you were the way you were. Knowing what you went through with your dad and all you had endured and seeing how much you have changed gives me hope and something to strive for. Moms, you have always been solid, never wavering one way or another. You have been the anchor that kept us rooted. You have also been the wind that kept this family moving, and the glue that kept us together. Jamal my brother, what can I say bro. I know you thought that I was the stand-out and the one who was always in front but real talk you were always that one. I had to do something because there was this quiet strength that you had. You didn't say much but when you did it was impactful and powerful. There was and still is a quiet confidence in you that makes you special. You have always been your own man not afraid to be different. I love you bro and appreciate everything that you have done for me. I just hope and pray that one day I can make you all proud as you have made me proud.

Well with that being said Mom, Pop, Aaron I have decided to stick around for a while. You are now looking at one of the new associates at Brooks and Mays Law Firm. They have set me up with Jasmine's old spot and everything is official as of today. There was even talk about me maybe starting another division sometime in the future if I didn't want to stay here. That's further down the road though. Right now, I'm here. Team ROSE!

Royce Dixon Sr.

ALSO, BY
ROYCE DIXON SR.

HIDDEN FEELINGS

by Royce Dixon Sr. Publication Date: December 2, 2018

HIDDEN FEELINGS REVEALED: IS THERE MORE

by Royce Dixon Sr. Publication Date: June 18, 2023

BLESSED WHILE BROKEN

by Royce Dixon Sr. Publication Date: January 2, 2020

JOJO'S LEARNING ADVENTURES

by Royce Dixon Sr. Publication Date: February 15, 2021

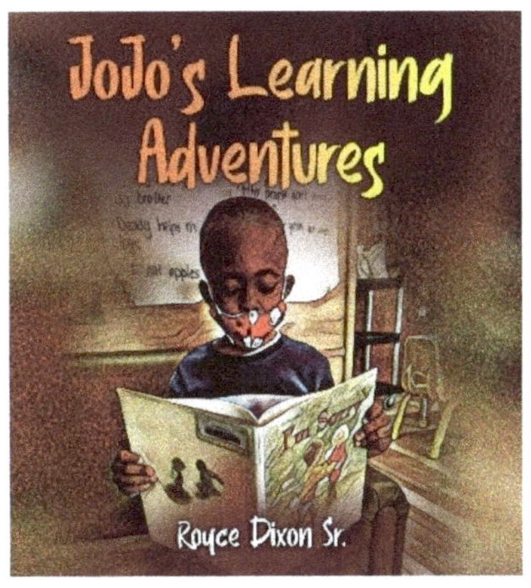

ABOUT THE AUTHOR: ROYCE DIXON SR.

Royce Dixon Sr. was born and raised in Rockford, Illinois, to Roy and Betty Dixon. He is the middle child of three, with an older sister, Karen, and a younger brother, Delvin. Royce's family plays a pivotal role in his life, offering love, support, and invaluable feedback. Their constant encouragement helps keep him grounded, motivated, and spiritually lifted.

Royce has been happily married for over 30 years to the love of his life, Lisa Dixon. Together, they have two children, Tracina and Royce II (TJ), and their close-knit family remains a source of inspiration and strength for him. They are central to his life and his work, with their support helping him navigate life's challenges and triumphs.

As a writer, Royce's location and cultural background significantly influence his work. Growing up in Rockford, he draws inspiration from the community, the courthouse, church, and neighborhood life. These environments provide him with a wealth of material to explore in his stories. His writing, which focuses primarily on fiction, is designed to inspire and bring hope to readers, with each story infused with heartfelt messages and life lessons.

Royce's literary journey has been marked by a number of significant milestones. Two of the most notable include being recognized as The Leading Man of SHE Publishing LLC for both 2023 and 2025. His writing career includes five published books: *Hidden Feelings, Blessed While Broken, JoJo's Learning Adventures, Hidden Feelings Revealed: Is There More*, and *A Rose on the Concrete Court*. His work is a reflection of his passion for storytelling and his desire to uplift others through his words.

A major inspiration for his latest book came from watching his younger brother, Delvin, evolve into a successful businessman. Royce takes great pride in witnessing Delvin's journey from his early years to the thriving individual he has become, demonstrating the power of perseverance, growth, and redemption.

In addition to Royce writing, he is the co-owner of Be Blessed Culture LLC, which encompasses Be Blessed Clothing and Be Blessed Photography. He and his wife Lisa also lead *I Still Do Ministries*, where they focus on helping couples cultivate stronger relationships and marriages. Their belief is that by strengthening relationships, they can contribute to better families, communities, and ultimately, a better society.

Outside of writing, Royce enjoys attending sporting events, taking photographs, spending quality time with his family, and engaging with people. His personal life is a testament to his belief in the importance of connection, love, and the power of community.

Through his work, Royce Dixon Sr. continues to inspire, motivate, and share his experiences, hoping to leave a lasting impact on those who read his stories.